"I Have Been Waiting For This."

Damon emphasized his words by running his hands up Madeline's arms. The heat of his palm warmed her skin. Electricity raced through her.

Judging from the quick flare of his nostrils, she wasn't the only one feeling the sparks.

He lowered his head and briefly sipped from her lips.

She didn't want to talk, didn't want to do anything to lessen the intoxicating effect of his lips and hands on her. She wound her arms around his neck and sifted his soft hair through her fingertips.

The waiting was over.

Dear Reader,

Like many American girls, I grew up hearing fairy tales and dreaming of my own prince. In my teens I switched to reading Harlequin Presents and Harlequin Romance novels, and just like the fairy tales of my childhood, those stories carried me away, filled me with hope and instilled in me a belief in happily ever after.

I hope you enjoy *The Prince's Ultimate Deception,* my modern-day version of Cinderella, as much as I enjoyed creating a magical kingdom and a prince worthy of his princess.

Happy reading,

Emilie Rose

P.S. Stop by my Web site at www.EmilieRose.com for updates on my books!

EMILIE ROSE

THE PRINCE'S ULTIMATE DECEPTION

Published by Silhouette Books

America's Publisher of Contemporary Romance

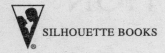

SILHOUETTE BOOKS

ISBN-13: 978-0-373-76810-3
ISBN-10:   0-373-76810-9

THE PRINCE'S ULTIMATE DECEPTION

Recent Books by Emilie Rose

Silhouette Desire

A Passionate Proposal #1578
Forbidden Passion #1624
Breathless Passion #1635
Scandalous Passion #1660
Condition of Marriage #1675
Paying the Playboy's Price #1732
Exposing the Executive's Secrets #1738
Bending to the Bachelor's Will #1744
Forbidden Merger #1753
**The Millionaire's Indecent Proposal* #1804
**The Prince's Ultimate Deception* #1810

*Monte Carlo Affairs

EMILIE ROSE

lives in North Carolina with her college sweetheart husband and four sons. Writing is Emilie's third (and hopefully her last) career. She's managed a medical office and run a home day care, neither of which offers half as much satisfaction as plotting happy endings. Her hobbies include quilting, gardening and cooking—especially cheesecake. Her favorite TV shows include *ER, CSI* and Discovery Channel's medical programs. Emilie's a country music fan, because she can find an entire book in almost any song.

Letters can be mailed to:
Emilie Rose
P.O. Box 20145
Raleigh, NC 27619
E-mail: EmilieRoseC@aol.com

To Christine Hyatt for sharing your wisdom
and showing me the path.
You helped me make my dreams come true.

One

"Please. You *have* to help me."

A woman's desperate plea caught Prince Dominic Andreas Rossi de Montagnarde's attention as he and his bodyguard Ian waited for the elevator inside Monaco's luxurious Hôtel Reynard. He observed the reflected exchange between a long-haired brunette and the concierge through the gilt-framed mirror hanging on the wall beside the polished brass elevator doors.

"Mr. Gustavo, if I don't get away from all this prewedding euphoria I am going to lose my mind. Don't get me wrong. I am happy for my friend, but I just can't stomach this much romance without getting nauseous."

Her statement piqued Dominic's curiosity. What had soured her on the fairy-tale fantasy so many others harbored? He had never met a woman who didn't wallow in wedding preparations. Each of his three sisters had dragged out the planning of their weddings for more than a year, as had his beloved Giselle.

"I need a tour guide who can work around my brides-maid's duties for the next month," she continued. "One who knows the best places for day trips and impromptu getaways because I don't know when I'll need to escape from all this—" she shuddered dramatically "—happiness."

American, he judged by her accent, and possibly from one of the Southern states given her slight drawl.

The concierge gave her a sympathetic smile. "I'm sorry, Mademoiselle Spencer, but it is nearly midnight. At this hour I cannot contact our guides to make those arrangements. If you will return in the morning I am sure we can find some-one suitable."

She shoved her fingers into the mass of her thick, shiny curls, tugged as if she were at her wit's end and then shifted to reveal an exquisite face with a classical profile. Her bare arms were slender, but toned, and she had a body to match beneath the floor-length green gown subtly draping her curves. Nice curves deserving of a second glance which Dom-inic willingly took. Too bad he couldn't see if her legs were as superb as the rest of her.

His gaze slowly backtracked to the reflection of her lovely face and slammed into mocking and amused emerald eyes the same shade as her dress. She'd caught his appraisal and repaid him in kind with a leisurely inspection of her own. Her gaze descended from his shoulders to his butt and legs. One arched eyebrow clearly stated she intended putting him in his place. He fought a smile over her boldness, but he couldn't prevent a quickening of his pulse. When her eyes found his once more he saw appreciation but no sign of recognition.

Interesting.

She returned her attention to the concierge. "In the morning I have to ruin two years' worth of dieting and exercise by stuffing myself with wedding cake samples. Please, I'm begging you, Mr. Gustavo, give me a guide's name tonight so I'll at least have the promise of escape tomorrow."

Escape. The word echoed in Dominic's head as he pondered the elevator's unusual slowness. He needed time to come to terms with his future, to marrying and having children with a woman he didn't love and might not even like, without the paparazzi shoving cameras in his face. In a word, he needed to escape—hence the lack of his usual entourage, dying his blond hair brown and shaving the mustache and beard he'd worn since he'd first sprouted whiskers.

This would in all likelihood be his last month of peace before all hell broke loose. Once the paparazzi caught wind of the proceedings at the palace they would descend on him like a plague of locusts, and his life would no longer be his own. He could see the headlines now. Widowed Prince Seeks Bride.

Apparently the American needed to escape, as well. Why not do so together? Looking at her would in no way be a hardship, and discovering how she'd willingly divorced herself from romance would be an added bonus.

He glanced at Ian. The bodyguard had been with him since Dominic's college days and sometimes Dominic swore the older man could read his mind. Sure enough, warning flashed in Ian's brown eyes and his burly body stiffened.

The elevator chimed and opened, but instead of stepping inside the cubicle Dominic pivoted toward the concierge stand. Ian hovered in the background, silently swearing, Dominic was sure. "Perhaps I could be of assistance, Gustavo."

Gustavo's eyebrows shot up, not surprising since the man often arranged Dominic's entertainment.

"Pardon me for eavesdropping, mademoiselle. I could not help but overhear your request. I would be happy to act as your guide if that meets with your approval?" Dominic waited for recognition to dawn in her eyes. Instead a frown pleated the area above her slim nose. From her smooth porcelain skin he guessed her to be in her late twenties or early thirties—far too young to have forsaken love. As was he. But what choice did he have when duty called?

Her gaze traveled over his white silk shirt and black trousers and then returned to his face. "You work here?"

Surprise shot through him. Was his simple disguise so effective? He had hoped to throw off the paparazzi from a distance, but he hadn't expected to fool anyone up close, and yet she apparently didn't know who he was. Admittedly, he'd lived as low profile a life as any royal could in the past few years, and he avoided the press more often than not, but still... Was this possible?

Dominic made a split-second decision not to enlighten her. He'd had a lifetime of cloying, obsequious women due to his lineage. Why not enjoy being a normal man for as long as it lasted? "I don't work for the hotel, but I am here as often as I can be. Hôtel Reynard is my favorite establishment."

She looked at Gustavo. "Can I trust him?"

Gustavo seemed taken aback by the question. As he should be. Dominic, as next in line to the throne of Montagnarde, a small three-island country four hundred miles east of New Zealand, wasn't accustomed to having his integrity questioned.

"*Certainement,* mademoiselle."

Her thickly lashed emerald gaze narrowed on Dominic's. "Are you familiar with Southern France and Northern Italy?"

His favorite playgrounds, and in recent years, prime examples of the types of tourist meccas he intended to develop in his homeland. "I am."

"Do you speak any languages other than English, because

I barely scraped by in my college Latin class, and I only know health-care Spanish."

"I am fluent in English, French, Italian and Spanish. I can get by in Greek and German."

Her perfectly arched eyebrows rose. Amusement twinkled in her eyes and curved her lips, rousing something which had lain dormant inside him for many years. "Now you're just bragging, but it sounds like you're just the man I need, Mr.…?"

He hesitated. To continue the masquerade he'd have to lie openly not just by omission and he detested liars. But he wanted to spend time with this lovely woman as a man instead of a monarch before fulfilling his duty and marrying whichever woman the royal council deemed a suitable broodmare to his stud service. What could it hurt? He and the American were but ships passing in the night. Or in this case, one small corner of Europe.

"Rossi. Damon Rossi." He ignored Gustavo's shocked expression and Ian's rigid disapproving presence behind him and extended his hand. Dominic hoped neither man would correct the hastily concocted variation of his name or his failure to mention his title.

"Madeline Spencer." The brunette's fingers curled around his. Her handshake was firm and strong and her gaze direct instead of deferential. When had a woman last looked him in the eye and treated him as an equal? Not since Giselle. Unexpected desire hit him hard and fast and with stunning potency.

A similar awareness flickered on Madeline's face, expanding her pupils, flushing her cheeks and parting her lips. "I guess that only leaves one question. Can I afford you?"

Caught off guard by her breathless query and by his body's impassioned response, Dominic glanced at Gustavo who rushed to respond for him. "I am sure Monsieur Reynard will cover your expenses, mademoiselle, since you are an *honored* guest of the family and a *dear friend* to his fiancée. Hi— Monsieur Rossi should not accept any money from you."

Dominic didn't miss the warning in Gustavo's statement.

Madeline's smile widened, trapping the air in Dominic's chest. "When can we get together to set up a schedule?"

If he weren't expecting a conference call from the palace with an update on the bridal selection process momentarily he would definitely prolong this encounter. "Perhaps tomorrow morning after your cake sampling?"

He realized he hadn't released her hand, and he was reluctant to do so. Arousal pumped pleasantly through his veins— a nice distraction from the disagreeable dilemma which had driven him into temporary exile.

Madeline was apparently in no rush, either, as she didn't pull away or break his gaze. "That'd be great, Damon. Where shall I meet you?"

Dominic searched his mental map for a meeting place not haunted by the paparazzi. The only option his testosterone-flooded brain presented was his suite, but the tour guide he'd implied himself to be could hardly afford penthouse accommodations. Already his lie complicated the situation.

Gustavo cleared his throat, jerking Dominic back to the present. "Perhaps *le café* located in the lower terrace gardens, Your—Monsieur Rossi?"

Dominic nodded his thanks—for the recommendation and for the conspiracy. He was used to being a leader and making decisions, but even a future king knew when to accept wise council. "A very good suggestion, Gustavo. What time will you finish, mademoiselle?"

Straight, white teeth bit into her plump bottom lip and Dominic struggled with a sudden urge to sample her soft pink flesh. "Elevenish?"

"I shall count the hours." He bent over her hand and kissed her knuckles. Her fragrance, a light floral mingled with the tart tang of lemon, filled his lungs, and his libido roared to life like the mythical dragon island folklore decreed lived beneath Montagnarde's hot springs.

Dominic had not come to Monaco with the intention of having a last dalliance before beginning what would in all likelihood be a passionless marriage. But he was tempted. Extremely tempted. However the lie, combined with his duty to his country meant he had nothing to offer this beautiful woman except his services as a guide. He would have to keep his newly awakened libido on a short leash.

It wouldn't be easy.

Madeline Spencer's fingers squeezed his one more time and then she released him with a slow drag of her fingertips across his palm. A sassy smile slanted her lips. "Until tomorrow then, Damon."

With a flutter of her ringless fingers she entered the penthouse elevator—the one he'd just abandoned. The doors slid closed.

Dominic inhaled deeply. For the first time in months the sword of doom hanging over his head lifted. He had a short reprieve, but a reprieve nonetheless.

"Oh. My. God." Madeline sagged against the inside of the penthouse suite door and pressed a hand over her racing heart. "I think I'm in lust."

Candace and Amelia, two of Madeline's three suite mates, straightened from their reclining positions on the sofas of the sitting room. They'd already changed from the evening gowns they'd worn to the casino earlier into sleepwear.

"With whom?" Amelia, wearing a ruffled nightgown, asked.

"I have just hired the most gorgeous man on the planet to be my tour guide."

"Tell all," Candace ordered. The bride-to-be was the reason Madeline, Amelia and Stacy, her bridesmaids, were sharing a luxurious suite in the five-star Hôtel Reynard. The quartet had been granted an all-expenses-paid month in Monaco compliments of Candace's fiancé, Vincent Reynard, to plan the couple's wedding, which would take place here in Monaco in four weeks.

"His name's Damon and he has the most amazing blue eyes, thick tobacco-brown hair and a body that won't quit. He's tall—six-three, I'd guess. It was nice to have to look up at a guy even when I was wearing my heels."

"Are you sure it's not *love* at first sight?" Amelia asked with a dreamy look on her face.

Madeline sighed over her coworker's die-hard romantic notions. "You know better. Love is not a fall I intend to take ever again."

Thanks to her lying, cheating ex-fiancé.

"Not all men are like Mike," Candace said as she stacked the tourist pamphlets she'd been perusing neatly on the table.

For Candace's sake Madeline hoped not. Vincent seemed like a nice guy and he truly doted on Candace. But Mike had done the same for Madeline in the early days, and therefore Madeline no longer trusted anyone carrying the Y chromosome.

"No, thank goodness, but my jerk detector is apparently broken, and there are enough guys out there like Mike that I've decided to focus on my career and avoid anything except brief, shallow relationships from now on. Men do it. Why can't I?"

Not that she'd had time for any kind of relationship lately, meaningless or otherwise, given the extra shifts she'd volunteered for at the hospital and the rigorous exercise program she'd adopted during the two years since Mike split.

"Sounds like you're hoping for more than guided tours from this guy," Candace guessed.

Was she? She couldn't deny the electricity crackling between her and Damon when they'd shaken hands, and when he'd kissed her knuckles her knees had nearly buckled. The man might be a tour guide, but he had class and charisma out the wazoo. She'd bet he could turn a shallow affair into a momentous occasion.

"Maybe I am. Maybe I want to have a wildly passionate vacation fling with a sexy foreigner. If he's not married, that is. He wasn't wearing a ring, but—" Their pitying expressions raised her defenses. "What?"

Amelia frowned. "This is about Mike showing up at the hospital last month with his child and pregnant wife in tow, isn't it?"

"It's not." *Liar.* But hey, a girl had her pride and Madeline planned to cling tightly to the ragged remnants of hers.

Mike had made a fool of her. He'd led her on with a six-year engagement, and then he'd dumped her on her thirtieth birthday when she'd jokingly suggested they set a wedding date or call it quits. As soon as he'd moved out of her town house and left his job as a radiologist at the hospital where they both worked, coworkers she'd barely known had rushed to inform her that while she'd been planning her dream wedding he'd been sharing his excellent bedside manner with other women. And judging by the family he'd brought by the E.R. last month, he'd married someone else and started pumping out babies as soon as he'd dumped her.

The lying, conniving rat.

Love? Uh-uh. Not for her. Never again. And she hoped reality didn't slap Candace in the face. But if that happened Madeline would be there to help her friend pick up the pieces—the way Candace and Amelia had been there for her.

Candace rose and crossed the room to wrap Madeline in a hug. "Just be careful."

Madeline snorted. "Please, I am a medical professional. You don't have to lecture me about safe sex. Besides, I'm on the Pill."

"I wasn't referring only to pregnancy or communicable diseases. Don't let that dickhead Mike make you do anything reckless you'll regret."

Candace and Amelia had never liked Mike. Maybe Madeline should have listened to her friends. But not this time. This time she wouldn't be blinded by love. This time she was looking out for number one. "That's the beauty of it. Assuming Damon is interested in a temporary relationship, he can't lead me on, dump me or break my heart because I'll be leaving right after the wedding. I mean, what can happen in four weeks?"

Amelia winced. "Don't tempt fate like that."

Candace sighed. "I know each of us has different things we want to see and do in Monaco, but don't spend all of your time with him. We want to see some of you, too."

Madeline bit her lip and studied her friend. How could she explain that being immersed in all the wedding hoopla brought back too many painful memories—memories of planning her own aborted wedding and wallowing in every intricate detail to make the day perfect? All for naught. She couldn't, without hurting Candace's feelings.

"I promise I won't abandon my friends or my bridesmaid's duties—no matter how good Damon is at guiding or anything else."

She looped an arm around each woman's waist. "Friends are forever and lovers—" she shrugged "—are not."

Good grief, she was as nervous as a virgin on prom night, and at thirty-two Madeline hadn't seen either virginity or prom night in a *long* time.

Her heart beat at double time and it had nothing to do with the sugar rush from sampling too many wedding cakes this morning.

Was her hair right? Her dress? And wasn't that just plain ridiculous? Nonetheless vanity had caused her to pull on a dress with a deep V neckline in the front and back and to don the outrageously sexy shoes she'd bought at the designer outlet down the street. She'd even French braided her unruly hair and added her favorite silver clip.

She scanned the partially open-air café for Damon. He rose from a table in the shadowy back corner, looking absolutely delicious in dark glasses, a casual, short-sleeved white cotton shirt and jeans. Wide shoulders. Thick biceps. Flat abs and narrow hips. Yum.

The glasses were a tad affected given he wasn't seated in the sunny section of the café, but so many people in Monaco sported the same look that he didn't seem out of place. Still— she tipped back her head and looked up at his handsome face—she'd rather stare into his pale blue eyes than at her own reflection.

"*Bonjour,* Mademoiselle Spencer." He pulled out her chair.

She tried to place his accent and couldn't, which was pretty odd since her job exposed her to an assortment of nationalities on a daily basis. And then there was the intriguing way he occasionally slipped into more formal speech….

"Good morning, Damon, and please call me Madeline." His knuckles brushed the bare skin between her shoulder blades as he seated her. Awareness skipped down her spine, startling a flock of butterflies in her stomach. *Ooh* yeah. Definitely a prime candidate for her first string-free fling.

She tugged a pen and pad of paper from her straw purse. "I thought we'd discuss possible outings today. Perhaps you could give me a list of suggestions, and I'll tell you which ones interest me."

"You will not trust my judgment to choose for you?"

As she'd done with Mike?

"No. I'd prefer to be consulted. I'm not sure how much you overheard last night, but I'm here with a friend to help plan her wedding. I'll have to be available for her morning meetings Monday through Friday and whenever else she or the other bridesmaids need me. So you and I will have to snatch hours here and there and not every day. Are you okay with that?"

"I am." He leaned back in his chair and steepled his fingers beneath his square jaw. He really had wonderful bone structure. His blade-straight nose had probably never been broken, and his high zygomatic arches allowed for nice hollows in his lean, smooth-shaven cheeks. Straight, thick, dark hair flopped over his forehead, making him look boyish, but the fine lines beside his eyes and mouth said he had to be in his thirties.

"Last night you said romance made you nauseous. I have yet to meet a woman who did not revel in romance. What happen—"

"Now you have," she interrupted.

His lips firmed and his eyebrows lowered as if her interruption annoyed him, but her sorry love life was not up for discussion.

The last thing she wanted to tell a prospective lover was that she'd been an idiot. She'd been so enthralled with the idea of love and being part of a couple that she'd given in to whatever Mike wanted, and in the process she'd surrendered part of her identity. What ticked her off the most was that even though she'd been trained to assess symptoms and make diagnoses, she'd missed the obvious signs that her relationship was in trouble. Not even the twenty pounds she'd gained over six years while "eating her stress" had clued her in to her subconscious's warnings.

"What happened to make you so wary?" he asked in a firm voice that made it clear he wasn't going to drop it.

She stared hard at him for several moments, trying to make him back down, but he held her gaze without wavering. "Let's just say I learned from experience that planning a perfect wedding doesn't always result in happily ever after."

"You are divorced?"

"Never made it to the altar. Now, about our excursions… Despite what Mr. Gustavo said about Vincent Reynard picking up your tab, I don't want to go overboard with expenses."

"I will keep that in mind. Are you more of an outdoor person or the museum type?"

She said a silent thank-you that he accepted her change of subject. "I prefer to be outside since I spend most of my waking hours inside."

"Doing…?"

Who was interviewing whom here? He didn't act like any potential employee she'd ever questioned. He was a little too arrogant, a little too confident, a little too in charge. But that only made him more attractive. "I'm a physician's assistant in a metropolitan hospital. What kinds of outings do you suggest?"

"There are numerous outdoor activities within a short distance that would cost little or nothing. Sunbathing, snorkeling, sailing, windsurfing, hiking, biking, fishing and rock climbing."

He ticked off the items on long ringless fingers bearing neatly trimmed, clean nails. She had a thing about hands, and his were great, the kind she'd love to have gliding over her skin.

"If you have more than a few hours we can go river rafting or spelunking in the Alpes-Maritimes or drive across the border into Italy or France to explore some of the more interesting villages."

"I'm not a sun lizard. Isn't that what they call the people who lay on the rocks of the jetty? I prefer action to lazing about, and cold, dark places give me the creeps, so let's skip the sunbathing and the spelunking and go with everything else. You'll arrange the tours and any equipment rental and provide me with the details?"

"It will be my pleasure."

She'd bet he knew a thing or two about pleasure, and if she was lucky, he'd share that knowledge. She slid a piece of paper across the table. "Here's my tentative schedule for the next month. I've blacked out the times when I'm unavailable. That's my suite number in the top corner. You'll have to call me there or leave a message for me at the front desk since my cell phone doesn't work in Europe."

She couldn't remember the last time she'd gone somewhere without a pager or cell phone, usually both, clipped to her clothing, and she couldn't decide whether she felt free or naked without the familiar weight bumping her hip.

A breeze swept into the open-air café, catching and ruffling the paper. She flattened her hand over it to keep it from blowing away. Damon's covered hers a split second later as he did the same. The heat of his palm warmed her skin. Electricity arced up her arm. Judging by the quick flare of his nostrils, she wasn't the only one feeling the sparks, but she couldn't see his eyes to be sure and that frustrated her.

She tilted her head, but didn't withdraw her hand. He didn't smile as he slowly eased his away, dragging his fingers the length of hers and igniting embers inside her.

"You know, Damon, if you're going to flirt with me it would be much more effective without the glasses. Hot glances don't penetrate polarized lenses."

He stilled and then deliberately reached up to remove his sunglasses with his free hand. "Are you interested in a flirtation, Madeline?"

The one-two punch of his accented voice huskily murmuring her name combined with the desire heating his eyes quickened her pulse and shortened her breath. "That depends. Are you married?"

"No."

"Engaged?"

"I am not committed to anyone at this time."

"Gay?"

He choked a laugh. "Definitely not."

"Healthy?"

His pupils dilated. He knew what she meant. "I have recently received a clean bill of health."

Excitement danced within her. "Then, Damon, we'll see if you have what it takes to tempt me."

Two

"This is a mistake, if I may say so, Dominic." Only in the privacy of their suite did Ian dare use Dominic's given name. Seventeen years together had built not only familiarity, but friendship.

"Damon. Damon Rossi," Dominic corrected as he packed for his first outing with Madeline Spencer.

"How am I to remember that?"

"D.A. Rossi is the name I sign on official documents, including the hotel registration. Damon is but a combination of my initials and an abbreviation of our country."

"Clever. But if the paparazzi catch you with a woman on the eve of your engagement…"

"As of this morning there is no engagement. A woman has not been selected, and if the council continues to argue as they have done for the past four months over birthing hips, pedigrees and whatever other absurd qualities they deem necessary for a princess, they will never come to an agreement, and I will not be forced to propose to a woman I know or care nothing about."

The council members had dehumanized the entire process. Not once had they asked Dominic's preferences. They might as well be choosing animals to breed from a bloodline chart.

Dominic had been nineteen when the council had chosen Giselle as his future bride, and he had not objected for he'd known her since they were children. His parents and hers had been friends for decades. He had convinced their families to postpone the marriage until after he obtained his university degree, and in those intervening years he and Giselle had become friends and then lovers before becoming husband and wife.

In the nine years since her death he had not met one single woman who made an effort to see the man behind the title and fortune.

And now once again the council would decide his fate as the traditions of his country decreed, a circumstance which did not please him, but one he was duty-bound to accept. But this time the idea of the group of predominantly old men choosing a stranger to be his wife did not sit well.

Dominic threw a change of clothing on top of the towels, masks and fins already in his dive bag. "Mademoiselle Spencer wishes to see Monaco. I wish to explore the tourist venues as a vacationer instead of as a visiting prince. Perhaps I will see a different side to the enterprises than I have seen before. The knowledge will benefit Montagnarde's tourist development plan which, as you know, I will present to the economic board again in two months. This time I will not accept defeat. They will back my development plan."

He had spent the years since he'd left university studying successful tourist destinations and laying the groundwork to replicate similar enterprises in his homeland. He wanted to model Montagnarde's travel industry after Monaco's, but the older members of the board refused to accept that the country had to grow its economic base or continue to lose its youth to jobs overseas. His father had sworn to lend his support in return for Dominic agreeing to marry before the end of his thirty-fifth year. With sovereign backing Dominic's plan would be passed.

"You know nothing about this woman," Ian insisted.

"A circumstance I am sure you have already begun to rectify." Any acquaintance with whom Dominic spent more than a passing amount of time was thoroughly investigated.

"I have initiated an inquiry, yes. Nevertheless, an affair would not be wise."

"Not an affair, Ian. A harmless flirtation. I cannot have sex with a woman to whom I am lying."

We'll see if you have what it takes to tempt me.

His heart rate quickened at the memory of Madeline's enticing banter and vibrant eyes. He would very much like to be her lover, but for the first time in years he found himself savoring the idea of being merely a man whom a beautiful woman found attractive. He didn't want to ruin that unique experience by revealing his identity, but he couldn't sleep with Madeline until he did. "I am aware of the risks."

"How will you explain my presence?"

Dominic zipped the bag and faced Ian, knowing his decision would not be a popular one. "The Larvotto underwater reserve is well patrolled by the Monaco police. No other boats or watercraft are allowed in the area. You can rest easy knowing the only dangers I face while snorkeling are that of the fish and the artificial reef. You will wait on the shore and keep your distance."

"I am charged with your well-being. If something should happen—"

"Ian, I have not given you reason to worry about my safety in years, and I won't now. I am a skilled diver. I have tracking devices in my watch and my swim trunks, and no one knows our plan. I will be fine." He hefted the bag. "Now come. I wish to see if Mademoiselle Spencer looks as good in a swimsuit as I anticipate."

Getting practically naked with a guy on your first date certainly moved things right along, Madeline decided as she removed the lemon-yellow sundress she'd worn as a cover-up over her swimsuit and placed it on the lounge chair beside her sandals and sunglasses.

Her black bikini wasn't nearly as skimpy as the thong suits so popular on the public beach around them. She scanned the sunbathers, shook her head and smothered a smile. The women here thought nothing of dropping their tops on the beach, but they didn't dare lie in the sun without their jewels. *Bet that makes for some interesting tan lines.*

To give him credit, Damon had stalked right past the bare breasts on display without pause. When his attention turned to her, raking her from braid to garnet-red toenail polish, she said a silent thank-you for the discounted gym membership the hospital offered its employees and the sweat and weight she'd shed over the past two years. Her body was tight and toned. It hadn't always been. But she wished Damon would lose the sunglasses. The thinning of his lips and the flare of his nostrils could signify anything from disgust to desire. She needed to see his eyes.

In the meantime, she did a little inspecting of her own as he untied the drawstring waist of the white linen pants he'd worn over his swimsuit due to Monaco's strict rules about no beachwear, bare chests or bare feet on the streets.

Damon's white T-shirt hugged well-developed pectorals and a flat abdomen. And then he dropped his pants. *Nice.* His long legs were deeply tanned, muscular and dusted with burnished blond hair beneath his brief trunks. "You must spend a lot of time outdoors."

He paused and gave her a puzzled look.

"The sun has bleached your body hair and the tips of your lashes," she explained.

"I enjoy water sports." He handed her a snorkel, mask and fins that looked new. "You have snorkeled before?"

"Yes, off the coast back home."

"And where is home?"

"North Carolina. On the eastern coast of the U.S. I live hours from the beach, but I used to vacation there every summer." She missed those boisterous vacations with Mike's family more than she missed Mike. The devious, dishonest rat. How could such a great family spawn a complete schmuck?

She dug her toes into the fine grains beneath her feet. "Is it true that all this white sand is brought in by barge?"

"Yes. That is the case for many of the Riviera beaches. Of the nations bordering the Mediterranean Sea, Monaco has the cleanest and safest beaches because the government is the most eco-conscious. Thanks to the Grimaldi family, the country is almost pollution free. In recent years the government has expanded its territory by reclaiming land from the sea. The underwater reserve we are about to explore was built in the seventies to repair the damage of overfishing and excessive coral gathering. The reefs are home to many fish species and red coral." He indicated the water with a nod. "Shall we?"

He'd certainly studied his guidebook. "Don't you want to take off your T-shirt?"

He tossed his shades on the chair beside hers. "No."

"Do you burn easily? I could put sunscreen on your back." Her palms tingled in anticipation of touching him.

"I prefer to wear a shirt, thank you."

Did he have scars or something? "Damon, I see shirtless men at work every day. If you're worried that I can't control myself…"

His chest expanded, and this time she received the full effect of those hot blue eyes. Arousal made her suck in her breath and her stomach. "It is not your control I question, Madeline. Come, the reef waits."

She'd never get used to the way he said her name with a hint of that unidentifiable accent. It gave her goose bumps every time. And speaking of control, where was hers? She wanted to jump him. Here. Now. "Where did you say you were from?"

"I did not say." He flashed a tight white smile and strode toward the water, where he dunked his fins and mask before donning both.

She mimicked his actions and then stared at him through the wet glass of her mask. "You like being a man of mystery, eh?"

He straightened and held her gaze. "I like being a man. The mystery is all in here." He gently tapped her temple. "Stay close to me. Watch for jellyfish and sea urchins. Avoid both."

Admiring the view of his taut buttocks and well-muscled legs, she followed him deeper into the water. For the next hour she swam and enjoyed the sea life. Each time Damon touched her to draw her attention to another sight she nearly sucked the briny water down her snorkel. Miraculously, she managed not to drown herself. By the time he led her back to shore her nerves were as tightly wound as the rubber band ball the emergency room staff tossed around on slow nights.

"That was great. Thanks." And then she got a good look at the shirt adhered like shrink-wrap to his amazing chest, the tiny buttons of his nipples and his six-pack abs. An even better sight and definitely one she'd like to explore.

"I'm glad you enjoyed it." He dropped his mask and fins on the chair, donned his sunglasses and ruffled his hair to shake off the excess water and then finger-combed the dark strands over his forehead.

"What made you decide to become a tour guide?" She dried off as he bagged their diving gear.

"When a country has few natural resources and limited territory, its people and the tourism industry become its greatest assets."

Surprised by his answer, she blinked. She'd expected a simple response such as he enjoyed meeting new people or the flexible hours, not something so deep. "Studied that, have you?"

"Yes."

She dragged her knit sundress over her head. "Where? I mean, are there tourism schools or what?"

Holding her gaze—or at least she thought he was, beneath those dark lenses—he hesitated so long she didn't think he'd answer. "I have a Travel Industry Management degree from the University of Hawaii at Mānoa."

He seemed tense, as if he expected her to question his statement, and she should. If he had a college degree and spoke four languages fluently then why was he acting as a tour guide? It didn't make sense. She reminded herself that not everyone was as career driven as she was, but Damon didn't seem the type to kick back and let the fates determine his future. She'd seen enough type A guys to recognize the signs and he waved them all like flags. But that was his business. A string-free affair—if they had one—didn't give her the right to interfere.

"The States? No kidding. What brings you to Monaco?"

"I am studying their tourism industry."

"And then what?"

"I'll apply what I've learned to my future endeavors." He zipped the dive bag and grabbed the handles. Eager to go, was he? Before she could ask what kinds of endeavors, he said, "If we leave now we'll have time to stop at the hotel café for a snack before I leave you. You have missed lunch."

"I'm in no rush. I had hoped we could spend the rest of the afternoon together. Maybe play some beach volleyball or jump on the trampoline at the far end of the beach? And this place is surrounded by restaurants. We could grab a bite here."

"I have another appointment."

She tried to hide her disappointment. While she had enjoyed the day, it hadn't gone quite as she'd hoped. Admittedly, she wasn't a practiced seductress, but if she wanted a vacation romance it looked as though she'd have to work harder for it.

Time to initiate Plan B. First she freed and finger-combed her hair while trying to build up her courage, and then she reached beneath her dress, untied her damp bikini top and pulled it through the scooped neckline.

A muscle at the corner of Damon's mouth ticked and his throat worked as he swallowed.

"You may change in one of the dressing rooms, as I will," he said hoarsely. His Adam's apple bobbed as he swallowed.

"No need. Besides, I didn't bring a change of clothing." Her nipples tightened when he didn't look away. Well, *hallelujah*. He'd been so professional and distant she'd begun to think she'd imagined the sparks between them.

And then in an act more brazen than anything she'd ever dared, she reached beneath her dress and shucked her bikini bottom. She twirled the wet black fabric once around her finger before tucking it along with her top in her tote. *Take that, big guy.* If Damon insisted on hustling her back to the hotel and dumping her, then he'd have to do so knowing she was naked except for a thin knit sheath.

Never let it be said that Madeline Spencer wouldn't fight for what she wanted, and in her opinion, Damon Rossi was the perfect prescription to mend her bruised ego and heart. A few weeks with him and she'd return home whole and healed.

"I wonder what all the commotion's about?"

Madeline's question pulled Dominic from his complicated calculations of hotel occupancy rates as the taxi approached Hôtel Reynard. He'd been attempting to distract himself from the knowledge that she was completely nude beneath her dress and failing miserably.

A camera-carrying group of a dozen or so paparazzi stood sentry across the street from the hotel with their zoom lenses trained on the limo parked by the entrance. Dominic silently swore. His escape route had been sealed. He leaned forward to speak to the driver. "Rue Langlé, *s'il vous plaît.*"

Madeline's eyebrows rose in surprise. "Where are we going?"

"I do not wish to fight the crowd. We'll dine in a quiet café instead of the hotel." Ian would not like the unplanned detour, and Makos, the second bodyguard who kept in such deep cover that Dominic rarely spotted him, would like it even less.

"I thought you were in a hurry to get to another appointment."

"It can wait." There was no other appointment. He merely needed time away from the tempting woman beside him before he grabbed her and kissed that teasing smile from her lips. Even in the cool water, touching the wet silkiness of her skin had heated his blood. He'd wanted to flatten his palms over her waist, tangle his legs with her sleek limbs and pull her flush against him. A maneuver that probably would have drowned them both, he acknowledged wryly.

Dominic faced a conundrum. With each passing moment his desire for Madeline increased, and yet his lie stood between them. He ached for her, but he was reluctant to lose the unique relationship they had established. She looked at *him*, flirted with *him*, desired *him*. Not Prince Dominic. He was selfish enough to want to enjoy her attentions a while longer.

She twisted in her seat to stare out the taxi's back window at the paparazzi as the driver took the roundabout away from the hotel. The shift slid her hem to the top of her thighs. A few more inches and he'd see what her bikini bottom should be covering. He gritted his teeth and fisted his hands against the urge to smooth his palm up her sleek thighs and over her bare buttocks.

"It's probably just another celebrity," she said. "Amelia says the hotel is crawling with them."

"Who is Amelia?"

"My friend and one of the other bridesmaids. She's a huge fan of entertainment magazines and shows. She claims the security inside the hotel makes it a celebrity hot spot. Supposedly paparazzi aren't even allowed on the grounds, which would explain why they're staked out across the street."

He'd have to avoid her friend. "You are not interested in star gazing?"

She settled back in the seat and faced him. "No. I don't have time to watch much TV or read gossip rags. I work four or five twelve-hour shifts each week, depending on how much overtime the hospital will allow me, and I usually go to the gym for another hour after work."

That could explain why not even a flicker of recognition entered her eyes when she looked at him—not that he was a household name, but he was known unfortunately, thanks to a couple of wild years after Giselle's death when he'd tried to smother his grief with women and parties. "Your diligence at the gym shows."

She tilted her head, revealing the long line of her throat and the pulse fluttering rapidly at the base. "Is that a compliment, Damon?"

"I am sure you are aware of your incredible figure, Madeline. You do not need my accolades." The words came out stiffly.

Her eyebrows dipped. "Are you okay?"

"Shouldn't I be?"

"You seem a little…tense."

His gaze dropped pointedly to her hiked hem.

She glanced down and her eyes widened. A peachy glow darkened her cheeks, making him question whether the siren role was a new one for her. And then the hint of a smile curved her lips as she wiggled the fabric down to a more respectable level. The woman was driving him insane and relishing every moment of his discomfort.

"Monaco is small enough that we could have walked to the café, you know," she said.

"You have had enough sun." And he was less likely to be recognized in an anonymous taxi. The driver pulled over in the street and stopped. Dominic paid him and opened the door. He noted Ian climbing from a taxi a half a block away. Dominic subtly angled his head toward the Italian café as a signal.

Madeline curled her fingers around Dominic's and allowed him to assist her from the car. She joined him on the sidewalk, but didn't release his hand. The small gesture tightened something inside him. When had he last held hands with a woman? Such a simple pleasure. One he hadn't realized he'd missed.

She tipped back her head. "Monaco has strict protocol. Are you sure we're dressed appropriately?"

One of us is. He had pulled on trousers and a polo shirt before leaving the beach. His attire was acceptable, as was Madeline's if one was unaware she wore nothing beneath the thin yellow sundress. The driver retrieved the dive bag from the trunk. Dominic took it from him. "The café is casual. I recommend the prosciutto and melon or the bruschetta."

He'd prefer to feast on her, on her rosy lips, on her soft, supple skin, on the tight nipples pushing against her dress.

Wondering when his intelligence had deserted him, Dominic led her inside and requested a table in the back. Madeline didn't release his hand until he seated her. He chose a chair facing away from the door. The fewer people who saw his face the better and Ian would cover his back.

The entire afternoon had been an exercise in restraint and a reminder that he was not an accomplished liar. He had been so distracted by his unexpected attraction to Madeline that he had almost blown his cover. Had she not commented on his blond body hair he would have removed his shirt and his secret would be out.

Your secret is keeping her out of your bed.

Without a doubt, he desired Madeline Spencer, but getting women to share his bed had never been difficult. Getting one to see him as a mere man, however, was nearly impossible. He would have to reveal his identity soon for he did not think his control would last much longer, and then if he could be certain Madeline could be happy with a short-term affair, he would explore every inch of her. Repeatedly.

But before he revealed *his* secret he needed to discover *hers*. Why had she renounced love?

After placing their orders Dominic asked, "Did you love him?"

Her smile wobbled and then faded. Her fingers found and tugged one dark coil of hair. He wanted to wind the spirals around his fingers, around his—

"Who?"

Her pretended ignorance didn't fool him. The shadows darkening her eyes gave her discomfort away. He removed his sunglasses and looked into her eyes. "The man who disappointed you."

She fussed with her cutlery. "*Pfft*. What makes you so sure there is one?" When he held her gaze without replying she bristled. "Is this twenty questions? Because if it is, you'll have to give an answer for every one you get."

Risky, but doable if he chose his words carefully. He nodded acceptance of her terms. "Did you love him?" he repeated.

"I thought I did."

"You don't know?"

She shifted in her seat, reminding him of her nakedness beneath the T-shirt thin layer of cotton. "Why don't you tell me what you have planned for our next outing?"

"Because you are a far more interesting topic." His voice came out in a lower pitch than normal as if he were dredging it up from the bottom of the sea. "Why do you question your feelings?"

She sighed. Resignation settled over her features. "My mother was forty-six when I was born and my father fifty.

They were too old to keep up with a rambunctious child. I wanted to do things differently when I had children, so I made a plan to get married and start my family before I turned thirty. I met Mike right after college. He seemed like the perfect candidate and we got engaged. But it didn't work out."

"One failed relationship soured you?"

Another squirm of her naked bottom made him wish he could take the place of her chair. "My parents divorced. It wasn't pretty. Have you ever been in a long-term relationship?"

"Yes."

Her arched brows rose. "And?"

"My turn. Why did your relationship end?"

She frowned. "Lots of reasons. First, I spent too much time trying to be the woman I thought he and society expected me to be instead of the one I wanted to be. Second, he found someone else."

"He is a fool."

A smile twitched her lips. "Don't expect me to argue with that brilliantly insightful conclusion."

The waitress placed their meals on the table and departed.

"Have you ever been married?" Madeline asked before biting into her bruschetta.

"Yes."

Her body stilled and her emerald gaze locked with his. She chewed quickly and then swallowed. "What happened?"

"She died." The words came out without inflection. He'd learned long ago to keep the pain locked away behind a wall of numbness.

Sympathy darkened her eyes. "I'm sorry. How?"

"Ectopic pregnancy."

She reached across the table and covered his hand. Her touch warmed him and surprisingly, soothed him. "That must have been hard, losing your wife and child at the same time. Did you even know she was pregnant?"

How could this virtual stranger understand what those closest to him had not?

"Yes, it was hard, and no, we didn't know about the baby." It had infuriated him at the time that many had been more concerned with the loss of a potential heir to the throne than the loss of his wife, his friend, his gentle Giselle. Only recently had his anger subsided enough for him to agree to another marriage. If his sisters had produced sons instead of daughters, he probably never would have.

They finished the meal in silence. He waited until Madeline pushed her plate aside before asking, "You do not wish for another *affaire de coeur* or the American dream of a house with a white picket fence and two-point-something children?"

She straightened and put her hands in her lap. "No. I'm over my urge to procreate. It's time to focus on me. My wants. My needs. My career. I don't need a man to complete me. And I don't need marriage to find passion."

Passion. Arousal pulsed through him. "You can be happy with brief liaisons? Without love?"

"Absolutely. In fact, I prefer it that way. If I want to take a promotion, a trip or stay out late with my friends, then I don't have to worry about anyone's ego getting bent. So, Damon…" Her fingertips touched his on the table. "What you said on the beach about your control…? Losing it with me would not be a problem."

He inhaled sharply. Her meaning couldn't be clearer. She wanted a lover. And he would be more than happy to oblige. The question was should he reveal his identity beforehand, or since she wanted nothing more than a brief affair, did he have to reveal anything at all? Did he have to ruin this camaraderie? For he knew with absolute certainty that the knowledge would change their relationship.

He stood and dropped a handful of bills on the table.

Her hand caught his and the need to yank her into his arms surged through him. "You paid for the taxi. Shouldn't I get this?"

"No." He pulled back her chair. She rose and turned, but Dominic didn't back away. Her breasts brushed his chest. His palm curved over her waist. "I know of a back entrance to the hotel."

Her quick gasp filled his ears and temptation expanded her pupils. "What about your other appointment?"

His gaze dropped from her emerald eyes to her mouth. "Nothing is more important at the moment than tasting you."

Her tongue swiped quickly over her bottom lip and he barely contained a groan. "We could go to your place."

Again the lie complicated matters. He shook his head. "I share with another man."

She grimaced. "And I'm sharing a suite with the bride-to-be and two other bridesmaids. I have my own bedroom, but I wouldn't feel right taking a man to my room."

And he had to avoid her celebrity-watching friend. He clenched his teeth to dam a frustrated growl and laced his fingers through hers. He led her outside the restaurant, passing by Ian on a nearby bench. Dominic scanned the area, for there was one thing that couldn't wait. A narrow flower-lined alleyway beckoned. Dominic ducked in, pulled Madeline behind a potted olive tree and into his arms.

"Wha—"

His mouth stole the word from her soft lips. Desire, instantaneous and incendiary, raced through his bloodstream at the first taste of her mouth. He sought her tongue, stroked, entwined and suckled. Madeline's arms encircled his waist, pressing her lithe body flush against his.

Her flowers and lemon scent filled his nostrils and her warmth seeped deep inside him. He tangled the fingers of one hand in her silky curls, caressed the curve of her hips with the other and pressed the driving need in his groin against her stomach.

A horn sounded in the street, reminding him of where they were and the omnipresent possibility of paparazzi. Except for a few insane months, he'd spent a lifetime carefully avoiding the press, and yet Madeline made him forget. Reluctantly, he lifted his head.

Madeline opened dazed eyes and blinked her long, dark lashes. Her lips gleamed damp and inviting as she gazed up at him. "That was worth waiting for."

For the first time in ages Dominic felt like a man instead of a dynasty on legs or an animal expected to breed on command. "I will arrange privacy for our next outing."

Three

Pain burned Madeline's throat Thursday morning, but she'd be damned if she'd let Candace know it. She gritted her teeth into a bright smile.

Watching the *couturière* fuss and flutter around her petite blond friend reminded Madeline of the wedding dress her mother and aunts had sewn for her. The trio had dedicated a year to creating a gorgeous gown and veil with intricate seed pearl beading and hand-tatted lace. Neither would ever be worn.

It should have been a clue that Madeline's engagement was doomed when her dream dress included a full cathedral train, and yet Mike had claimed he wanted an informal backyard wedding, or better yet, a Vegas quickie—if she'd pay for the trip. Her fiancé had been loaded, and yet he'd been a total miser.

She shook off the memories and widened her smile. "You look gorgeous, Candace. That dress couldn't be more perfect if it had been custom-made for you."

"You think?" Her friend smoothed her hands over the silk douppioni skirt beneath a hand-beaded bodice and twisted this way and that to see her reflection in the three-way mirror. "I'm not showing?"

Another twinge of regret pinched Madeline's heart. If she'd stuck with her plan, she probably would have had several babies by now. But since Mike couldn't keep his pants zipped most likely they would have been divorced and playing tug-of-war with innocent children. Not a pretty picture. She ought to know. Her parents' divorce when Madeline was ten had been rough.

Breaking up with Mike had been for the best, and luckily his paranoia over the two percent failure rate of the Pill had led him to use condoms as a backup every single time. Otherwise, there was no telling what the two-timing louse would have brought home from his extramural adventures.

Candace's expectant expression dragged Madeline back to the present. "Candace, no one will know you're pregnant unless you tell them. The empire waist covers everything—not that there's anything to hide yet. You're only eight weeks along."

Candace had confided her pregnancy to Madeline and sworn her to secrecy before they'd left North Carolina. She'd wanted Madeline's medical assurance in addition to her obstetrician's that traveling in her first trimester wouldn't endanger the baby.

"Okay, this is the dress. *Je voudrais acheter cette robe,*" Candace told the seamstress.

The seamstress rattled off a quick stream of French while she unfastened the long line of silk-covered buttons down Candace's spine, and Candace replied in the same language. Madeline didn't have a clue what either of them said. She should have borrowed those French lesson CDs her suitemate Stacy had used.

The heavy fabric swished over her friend's head. With the dress draped over her arms, the seamstress departed. Candace quickly pulled on her street clothes, crossed the dressing room to Madeline's side and took her hands. "You had a lucky escape. You know that, right?"

Madeline winced. She should have known her friend would see through her fake merriment. They'd been through a lot together in the past twelve years: college, their engagements to Mike and Vincent and the deaths of Madeline's father and Candace's brother. "I know, and trust me, I am not missing that two-timing dud."

"But the wedding preparations are hard for you." It was a statement, not a question. "I'm sorry. But I couldn't do this without you, Madeline."

"I love seeing you this happy."

"Your turn will come." Candace squeezed her fingers and released her.

Not as long as I have a functioning brain cell. God forbid I ever go through that again. "This month is all about you."

"When will the rest of us get to meet your gorgeous guide?"

"I'm not sure. I'll have to ask. I won't see him again until Saturday." Two days. It seemed like an aeon.

After kissing her into a stupor yesterday Damon had put her in a cab with the promise of passion to come. If that kiss was a sample of what she could expect, then it would be passion unlike any she'd ever experienced. She couldn't remember Mike's embrace ever making her forget where she was.

Last night after dinner with Candace at the world-renowned Hôtel Hermitage she'd returned to the suite and found a message from Damon telling her he had arranged a sailboat for the weekend. He'd found a place for them to be alone. Her mouth dried, her palms moistened and her pulse bounded like a jackrabbit. She felt wild, reckless and free. A first for her.

"Maybe Damon will sweep you off your feet, and we'll have a double wedding in three weeks," Candace interrupted Madeline's illicit thoughts.

Madeline groaned. "Don't start your matchmaking here. It's bad enough that I suffer through your blind date matchups at home. Besides, I'd never be stupid enough to marry a guy I'd known such a short time."

She hitched her purse over her shoulder and opened the door, hoping Candace would leave the topic behind in the dressing room of the chic boutique.

Candace followed her out. "That's just it. When you love someone you don't want to wait. The only reason I waited to marry Vincent was because he insisted on being able to put the wedding ring on my finger himself. The day he reached that point in his physical therapy we set the date."

Which reminded Madeline of the crazy year her friend had had. Vincent had been severely burned along the right side of his body just over a year ago in a freak pit accident at the local race track. Madeline had treated him in the E.R. when he'd first arrived at the hospital and then Candace had been his nurse throughout his months-long stay in the burn unit. Before he'd been released the two had fallen head over heels in love.

Madeline had to give Vincent credit. He'd tried to convince Candace she deserved a man who wouldn't be scarred for life, but Candace didn't care about his scars. Love truly was blind.

A fact you know all too well.

Candace handed her credit card to the clerk and then turned back to Madeline. "The fact that you dated Mike for almost a year before you became engaged and you didn't push him to set a date for six years tells me you weren't in a rush to tie yourself to him till death do you part."

Good point. She hated it when others saw something that should have been obvious to her. "When did you become a shrink? I thought you were a nurse."

Candace shrugged. "Nurse. Shrink. Most days they're one and the same in the burn unit. But I don't need to be a psychiatrist to know that Mike didn't treat you well. You deserve a guy who will, Madeline."

"I'm strictly a love 'em and leave 'em gal from now on."

"That's a knee-jerk reaction to the dickhead's lies. You'll get over it, Ms. Monogamy. You're the one whose only lover was a man you thought you were going to marry."

Madeline's cheeks flashed hot. She glanced at the *couturière*. If the woman understood English—and most people in Monaco did apparently—she gave no sign of being interested in their exchange.

Having older parents meant Madeline's values were from a bygone era, and she'd waited to fall in love before falling into bed. But that was because her father had been a tough, no-nonsense vice squad detective with a habit of scaring off his teenage daughter's potential suitors and later she'd been too busy with school and a part-time job to have the energy to date.

But she had every intention of sowing the wild oats she'd been hoarding—starting with Damon Rossi. "My inexperience is a circumstance I intend to remedy as soon as possible."

"I still think there's more to your instant attraction to Damon than lust. I've never known you to get gaga so fast."

Madeline didn't reply until the shop door closed behind them. She faced her friend on the sunny sidewalk lined with designer shops and wrought iron lampposts. "Candace, I'm not gaga. I'm horny. And that's all it is. I have a two-year itch to scratch. Nothing more. Nothing less."

"Right. It took you ten months to sleep with Mike. You wanted to jump Damon after ten minutes. Listen to your subconscious, Madeline. It's trying to tell you something."

"You're wrong. Completely. Totally. Unequivocally wrong. And I'll prove it. Just watch."

She'd live it up in Monaco and then leave in three weeks' time with her sexual urges satisfied and her heart intact.

This had to be a mistake.

Madeline stopped on a long stretch of sunbaked dock in the Port de Monaco. Over a hundred boats bobbed and swayed around her in neat rows, and because it was Saturday, a number of other boaters were out and about, chatting in a musical chorus of foreign languages. The boats in this line were big. None resembled the small craft she'd expected Damon to rent. She double-checked the slip number on the note the hotel desk attendant had given her. Whoever had taken the message must have misunderstood.

No problem. She slung the strap of her beach bag over her shoulder and started walking. She'd check out slip one-eighteen just in case there was a smaller sailboat tucked behind the big ones. If there wasn't, she'd return to the hotel and wait for Damon to call with the correct instructions. Surely he'd guess something had gone awry when she didn't arrive on time?

Sun warmed her skin. Boat parts clanged and creaked beside her and birds cried overhead. A breeze teased tendrils from her braid and molded her skirt and cropped sleeveless top to her body. She'd only made it past a half-dozen yachts when a familiar dark-haired figure in white pants, a loose white shirt and sunglasses stepped onto the planks from a boat about five car lengths long. Her heart and steps faltered. The hotel hadn't made a mistake. Damon had rented a boat with a cabin. Make that a *yacht* with a cabin.

And because Candace didn't have a morning meeting tomorrow, Madeline was free to spend the night if she chose. She moved forward, one step at a time. Her lungs labored as if she'd sprinted from the hotel instead of ridden in the cushy hired car Damon had arranged for her. She'd never had a wildly passionate no-strings-attached affair, but if she boarded the boat, there would be no turning back.

This is what you wanted.

Maybe so, but that didn't keep her from being nervous. The distance between them seemed to stretch endlessly.

Damon didn't smile, didn't move toward her. Hands by his side and legs braced slightly apart, he waited, looking as if he belonged at a yacht club. But then she supposed a good tour guide should fit into his surroundings. He'd said he enjoyed water sports so he probably had the sea legs to handle a gently undulating dock and a boat that probably cost more than her condo.

She reached his side, shoved her sunglasses up onto her head and waited, poised on a knife edge between tension and anticipation. Her reflection in his dark lenses looked back at her, and his cedar and sage scent teased her nose.

She bit her lip and eyed the yacht. "I'm going to hate billing Vincent for this rental. I'll cover it. If I can afford it."

"The boat is borrowed. There is no charge." Damon took her bag. Their fingers touched and sparks swirled up her arm and settled in a smoldering pile in her stomach. His palm spread across the base of her spine, upping her body temperature by what felt like a dozen degrees. "Come aboard, Madeline."

Still, she balked. "It's only fair to warn you that I've never been on a sailboat. I don't know the bow from the stern."

A hint of a smile flickered on his lips. "You have nothing to fear. I won't ask anything of you that you're not willing to give. Our only task is to enjoy the sail and each other."

Her breath shuddered in and then out. He'd read her pretty easily. It wasn't the sail making her jittery. It was the prospect of being alone with him, of giving in to these foreign and over-whelming feelings and embarking on an uncharted sensual journey. "Okay."

He guided her onto the boat's back deck. A hip-high wall surrounded an area about ten feet square. He descended through a door into the cabin below and then turned and offered his hand. "Watch your step and your head."

Her fingers entwined with his and the heat of his palm spread through her making her knees shaky. At the base of the stairs she paused and blinked, allowing her eyes to adjust to the dimmer interior. Once she could focus, what she saw dazzled her. The luxury of stained wood cabinetry and bisque leather upholstery surpassed anything she'd ever seen—even her plush hotel suite.

Without releasing her hand Damon led her through a sitting area and a kitchen. He stepped through another door and moved aside for her to enter. A bed dominated the spacious stateroom—a bed she'd soon be sharing with him. Her heart thumped harder. The room seemed to shrink in size and the oxygen thinned. Her skin dampened, but her mouth dried.

Long, narrow horizontal windows let in sunlight, warming the cabin. Or maybe it was the knowledge of what lay ahead making her hot. She plucked at her suddenly clingy shirt.

"You may change in here or in the head." He dropped her bag on a bed and indicated a bathroom by tilting his head, and then he removed his sunglasses and tossed them on the mattress. Holding her gaze with desire-laden eyes, he cupped her shoulders. "Need help changing?"

"I, um…no." She swallowed the lump in her throat. She'd wanted adventure and she'd found it. Nerves, excitement and expectation vied for dominance inside her. Nerves won.

His hands coasted down her arms in a featherlight caress and then encircled her waist. He edged his fingers beneath the hem of her top and found the sensitive skin above her skirt. A shiver worked its way outward from the circles he drew on her abdomen with his thumbs. Mike's touch had never affected her this way—not even in the early days when the sex had been good.

"I have been waiting for this." He lowered his head and briefly sipped from her lips.

She didn't want to talk, didn't want to do anything to lessen the intoxicating effect of his lips and hands on her. She wound her arms around his neck and sifted his soft hair through her fingertips. "Me, too."

With a groan he pulled her closer, fusing the length of his body to hers and kissing her hungrily. His torso was hot and hard against hers, his tongue slick and skilled. A gentle tug on her braid tipped her head back, allowing him to delve deeper, kiss harder. Madeline held him close, savoring the sensations whirling through her. She clenched and unclenched her fingers in his hair and then swept her palms over his broad shoulders and down his back.

Footsteps above her startled her into jerking out of his embrace. "What's that?"

"Our crew is casting off. We'll stay below deck until we clear the harbor."

There were strangers on board? She'd thought they'd be alone. Uneasiness prickled her spine. "Why?"

"To stay out of their way while they navigate the channel."

"No, I mean why do we have a crew?"

"Because my attention will be focused on you and not on sailing. Change into your swimsuit and then join me in the galley." He swept his thumb over her bottom lip, grabbed his sunglasses and then left the room, closing the door behind him.

Madeline stared at the wooden panel. Her father had been overprotective—a hazard of his occupation dealing with the seamier side of life. Were his frequent warnings the cause of her uneasiness?

Lose the paranoia. Enjoy your weekend. It makes sense to have a crew on a boat this large, especially since you know nothing about sailing.

Tamping down her misgivings, she reached for her bag.

Seduction on the Mediterranean Sea. Damon had delivered nothing less in the hours since they'd left Monaco behind.

Madeline stood beside him on the front—*bow*—of the anchored sailboat with the deck rocking gently beneath her feet. She sipped her wine and feigned calm when every cell in her body quivered with eagerness for the night ahead. Lights on shore flickered on the ink-dark horizon. She didn't know from which city or even which country.

She turned her head and found Damon's blue gaze locked on her face in the pale moonlight. Sexual energy radiated from him. The entire day had been one long session of foreplay. She'd been wined and dined and tantalized from the moment she'd joined him in the kitch—*galley*. He'd massaged sunscreen into her skin and painted erotic designs on her body with the end of her braid. But he hadn't allowed her to return the favor. He'd kept his shirt on and insisted she keep her hands to herself. Whatever blemishes he was hiding beneath that fabric, she'd prove to him that they didn't matter.

Damon opened his mouth and took a breath as if preparing to speak, but closed it again as he'd done a few times today. He stared at the wine he swirled in his glass, finished it in one gulp and looked at her again.

He wasn't getting shy on her, was he? She never would have pegged him as the reticent type. But then what did she know about him except that he was drop-dead sexy, could drive her to the brink of orgasm without touching the usual parts and that the concierge trusted him?

She slipped an arm around his waist, rose on tiptoe and kissed his chin because she couldn't reach his lips. Damon dipped his head and covered her mouth, parted her lips and swept inside. He tasted like wine, sunshine and the promise of passion. And then he pulled away, cupped her face and pressed it to his shoulder. "Not here. Let's go below."

He laced his fingers with hers and quickly led her inside. There was no sign of Ian and Makos, the crew, in the sitting area or galley. The men must be in their cabin at the rear of the boat. Her worries about them had been unfounded. They'd efficiently done their jobs without encroaching on her and Damon's privacy although she'd been aware of their presence. How could she not be when both men were built like football defensive linemen?

Damon deposited their wineglasses on the counter before leading her into the bedroom at the front of the craft and closing the door behind them. Moonlight seeped through the narrow windows, bathing the room in silvery light. He didn't turn on the lamp and she wondered if that was because of the scars or whatever he hid under his shirt. She could scarcely hear the smack of the waves against the hull over her thundering heart.

Damon's expression turned serious and he seemed a little uneasy. He cupped her shoulders. "Madeline—"

She pressed her fingers to his lips. "It's okay. I'm nervous, too."

He opened his mouth to speak again, but she shook her head and traced his soft bottom lip with her fingertip. "Would you believe I am thirty-two years old and I've only had one lover?" His eyes widened and she cringed. "I'm not telling you that because I want a proposal or anything. I don't. This affair is about here and now and that's all. I just want you to know I might be…limited skillwise. But I'm a fast learner. Now please, kiss me. You've driven me insane all day. I want to do the same for you and I can't wait another second."

But he made her wait ten seconds before banding his arms around her and hauling her close. He took her mouth in a hard, hungry kiss, shifted his head and stole another and another until she clung to him because her legs no longer felt steady. She broke the connection to gasp for air. Their gazes locked and panted breaths mingled.

After a day of not being allowed to touch him, Madeline seized the opportunity to run her hands over him. His shoulder and arm muscles flexed beneath her fingers, and then she shaped his broad back, his narrow waist and finally, his tush. His groan vibrated over her like thunder. He splayed his hands over her bottom and yanked her against the ridge of his erection. Whatever deficiencies he thought he had, that wasn't one of them.

He shoved off the jacket she'd put on after dinner and then bunched the fabric of her top in his hands and whisked it over her head. Her white lace bra glistened in the moonlight and then with a flick of his fingers that, too, was gone and his warm hands shaped her breasts. With a whimper of delight, she closed her eyes and let her head fall back. Pleasure radiated from the nipples he buffed with his thumbs and coalesced into a tight, achy knot of need beneath her navel.

He dipped his head and circled her aureole with his tongue. Hot. Wet. Her knees weakened. She fisted her hands in his shirt and held on. And then he suckled and she whimpered as currents of desire swirled wildly inside her.

"Hurry. Please." She'd never been so aroused in all her life, and he'd barely touched her. She blamed it on the drawn-out foreplay of the day, his scent, his heat, his unique flavor. Her fingers fumbled on the buttons of his shirt, and then finally the last one separated and she pushed the shirt out of her way. The room was too dim to see more than a shadow of chest hair, but his muscles were taut and tight and rippled beneath her questing fingers. No raised or puckered scar tissue marred his supple skin. Nothing to be ashamed of. She found the fastening on his waistband.

He captured her other nipple with gentle teeth, hastily unzipped her skirt and pushed it to the floor. Frantic with need, she sent his shorts and briefs on the same path. She wanted him naked and inside her before she came without him. She'd never been a multiple-o's girl, and she wasn't wasting her one and only on a solo trip. His hand covered the satin front of her panties, stroked, teased. She clenched every muscle and fought off climax, but she was close, too close.

Slapping her hand over his to still him, she gasped, "Condoms. In my beach bag. Now."

His smile gleamed white in the near darkness. "Impatient?"

"Yes."

"I want to taste you."

"Next time. Please, Damon. I'm about to come unglued."

His smile vanished. He hesitated a second before reaching

for her beach bag and handing it to her. She dug until she found the new box of condoms, dropped her bag on the floor and ripped the box open. He reached to take the packet from her.

"No. My turn." She tore the wrapper and reached for him, encircling his thick erection with her fingers and stroking his hard, satiny length. A deep growl rumbled from him.

Mike, the twit, would have a serious case of penis envy if he knew how much better endowed Damon was.

But then Damon tweaked her nipples and thoughts of Mike evaporated in a hot rush of desire. She applied the protection, yanked the covers from the bed and scooted backward toward the headboard. Damon followed, crawling across the mattress like a stalking panther. Impatient for him to pounce, she shimmied her panties over her hips. Damon hooked them with his fingers and tugged them the rest of the way down her legs and tossed them over his shoulder.

"Loosen your braid." His raspy voice against the inside of her knee gave her goose bumps.

She did as he ordered. The moment she finished he plowed his fingers into her hair, cradled her head and devoured her mouth, demanding a response which she was more than happy to give. His body lowered over hers, and hot skin melded to hotter skin from her ankles to her nose. The sheer eroticism of his hair-spattered flesh against hers sent a shiver of delight over her. His masculine scent filled her nostrils, his taste made her crave more. She hooked a leg behind his hip. "Please."

He angled to the side. His fingers parted her curls, found her wetness. And then he did the unforgivable. With only three strokes he made her come. *Without him.* Damn it, she railed even as ecstasy convulsed her body and emptied her lungs.

Before she could protest he filled her with one deep thrust. She'd scarcely caught her breath before he withdrew and returned. Harder. Deeper. Again and again he pounded into her. Instead of relaxing and cooling down the way she usually did after climax, her heart continued to race and her muscles coiled tight again.

She couldn't. Could she?

Not believing what her body was telling her, she dug her nails into his hips and her heels into the mattress and urged him to go faster. And then it happened. Orgasm broke over her like the waves that had crashed over the bow this afternoon, sprinkling sensation on her skin like droplets of seawater.

Smiling with surprise and delight, she buried her face in his neck and then nipped his earlobe. Damon groaned against her temple. His back bowed and he thrust deeper as his climax shook him. And then he collapsed on top of her.

She savored his weight, his warmth, his sweat-slickened skin against her chest and beneath her palms. The sound of water smacking the hull slowly replaced the roar of her pulse.

"Wow," she whispered. "Thank you."

Damon braced himself on his elbows and lifted, his satisfied gaze locking with hers. "Good?"

"Oh yeah." Had her responsiveness been a fluke? She couldn't wait to find out. "Wanna do it again?"

Life didn't get any better than this.

With anticipation dancing across her skin Madeline opened the bathroom door and eased into the bedroom. She lifted a hand to shield her eyes from the blinding sunlight flooding through the cabin windows.

Damon rolled over looking smug, sexy and disheveled beneath the rumpled covers. He'd earned the right. They'd made love three times last night, and he'd made a multiple-o's girl out of her each time. In fact, he'd made her wish for a few fleeting moments that this could be more than just a vacation fling. She liked him, and the man was divine in bed.

His hungry gaze raked her nakedness, inflaming her and making her feel sexy, desired and special. He flipped back the sheet and patted the mattress. "Come here."

Something wasn't right. Madeline's steps faltered. The hair on Damon's head was a rich tobacco-brown, but the curls on his chest and surrounding his impressive erection were dark golden blond.

Like the beard stubble on his chin.

Like the hair on his arms and legs.

Not sun bleached.

Huh?

"You're a natural blond?"

Guilt flashed in his eyes. "Yes."

"Damon, why would you—"

He grimaced and shook his head. "Dominic. My name is Dominic. Not Damon."

Warning prickles danced along her spine. She wrapped her arms around her naked middle. "Your— What?"

"I can explain." He swung his long legs over the side of the bed, stood and stepped toward her.

She held up a hand to halt him and backed away from his rampant masculinity while she struggled with the facts. One corner of her mind registered that he had a body worthy of the cover of a fitness magazine or a centerfold, but the other...

"You lied to me?"

"Other than my name, everything I've told you is true."

The man who'd given her the most incredible night of her life was a liar?

Shades of Mike.

"You expect me to believe that?"

"Yes." He exhaled. "Madeline, I am sorry for the deception, but I wanted a chance to be with you as a man instead of—" his chin shifted, his shoulders squared and resignation settled over his face "—instead of a monarch."

Confused, she blinked. "As in 'butterfly?'"

A smile twitched his lips. "As in Prince Dominic Andreas Rossi de Montagnarde at your service." He bowed slightly.

"Huh?" What in the hell did that mean? He thought he was a prince? Was he certifiable?

His eyes narrowed as he straightened. "The name means nothing to you?"

"Should it?"

"My father is the King Alfredo of Montagnarde, a three-island nation in the South Pacific. I am next in line to the throne."

Fear slithered through her, making her heart blip faster. She was somewhere in the Mediterranean Sea at least a mile offshore with a delusional guy. "Sure you are. A prince, I mean."

Where were the survival instincts her father had drilled into her from an early age? Why had she ignored the warning prickles when she found out there were strangers on board? And why had she ignored the voice that said Damon was too good to be true?

Adrenaline flooded her veins, making her extremities tingle and her heart pound. Medical professionals called it the fight-or-flight response. Her father had called it live-or-die instinct, and he'd credited it with saving his life on more than one occasion. She'd put herself in danger, but she was going to get out of it. There was no other option.

Without taking her eyes off Damon, she reached for the skirt she'd discarded last night, yanked it on and zipped it. "Take me to shore."

"Madeline—"

"Now." She fumbled on her bra and then her shirt. Where had he thrown her panties? She couldn't afford to be vulnerable in any way, shape or form. She located the scrap of lace and donned it.

"I can't do that. Not yet."

She stilled and alarm raced through her. "Why not?"

"You must listen to me first. I wish to explain."

She didn't know why Damon had lured her onto a yacht, but she wished like the devil she'd paid more attention to the grim warnings of white slave trade and crime outside Monaco that Candace's future sister-in-law had shared along with etiquette lessons, but Madeline had written the woman off as an obsessed alarmist.

Wrong.

Inhaling deeply, she tried to recall what she'd been taught about handling unbalanced people and hazardous situations in the E.R. It didn't happen often, but there had been a few times when she'd had to protect herself and the other patients until security arrived.

Rule one: be aware of your surroundings. "Where are we exactly?"

"Off the coast of France."

Rule two: don't alarm the suspect. Keep him calm.

She forced a smile, but it wobbled. "Damon, I'd really like to go ashore."

"That's impossible. You don't have your passport."

Good point. But wouldn't the authorities understand just this once?

He moved closer. "Madeline—"

"Stop. Stop right there."

Rule three: when all else fails use the weapons at hand. There were knives in the kitchen. She'd seen them last night when she and Damon had prepared dinner together. Damon had cooked. What prince cooked? Royalty had servants for that kind of thing. Therefore, he was no prince.

She shoved her feet in her shoes, jerked open the cabin door and scanned the kitchen—*galley. Dammit, who cares what it's called?* She had to get off this boat. Ian and Makos sat at the table. Would they help her? Or were they in on this, too? She could take one guy. But three would be tricky.

She opened drawers until she found the one containing a razor-sharp filet knife with a nine-inch blade. And then Damon—Dominic…whatever the hell his name was—entered the small kitchen and reached for her. Using one of the self-defense moves her father had taught her she grabbed his right arm, ducked and turned and twisted his wrist up behind his back. She pressed the knife to his throat.

"Tell your friends to take me to shore. Now."

She heard an ominous sound and looked up to see two handguns pointed at her from across the room. Big, black ugly weapons. The crew members were in on this and armed.

My God. She was being kidnapped.

Four

"Ian, Makos, lower your weapons," Dominic stated calmly. Neither man complied. "That is an order."

"But Your Highness—" Ian protested.

"Do it. Madeline isn't going to hurt me." Dominic honestly believed it. He could feel the frightened quiver of her tense body pressed against his bare back and see the fine tremor of the hand at his jaw—the same hand that had brought him indescribable pleasure last night.

"That's what you think, buster. I'm a trained medical professional. I know where to cut to take you down instantly." The hand clamped around his wrist might not be completely steady, but her grip and voice were strong. She honestly believed her life was in danger—a circumstance he deeply regretted.

His bodyguards had lowered their guns, but raised them again upon hearing her threat.

Dominic subtly shifted a couple of inches to his right to

prevent the men from getting a clear shot at her. "Perhaps I should mention that Ian and Makos are my bodyguards. It is not wise to provoke them."

A slight shake of his head had the guards returning the weapons to the holsters concealed by their jackets with obvious reluctance.

He didn't doubt Madeline had the skill to kill him, but he doubted she had the nerve, and he wouldn't give her reason to find it. "If you incapacitate me, you will lose not only your human shield, but also your bargaining power. As a medical professional you took an oath to do no harm. Release me before someone gets hurt."

"Right." Disbelief colored the word. "And then what? You and your goons sell me? Ransom me? What?"

"I have no intention of ransoming or selling you. We'll return to port. Ian, give Madeline your phone so that she may call the hotel. Gustavo will vouch for me."

Her breasts nudged his back and her breath puffed against his nape as she snorted. "The concierge is probably in on this…this kidnap attempt. He told me I could trust you. If I call anyone, it'll be the police."

"You haven't been kidnapped. You boarded this yacht of your own free will as any of the other marina patrons will attest. And you will be returned unharmed. Call the authorities if you must, but doing so will be time consuming and embarrassing once the press gets involved."

"What press?"

"The ones I had hoped to avoid with my disguise. I colored my hair and shaved my beard because I wished to vacation without being hunted by the paparazzi. That's why I avoided the hotel after our swim at Larvotto. I did not wish to be recognized by predators with telephoto lenses."

A half minute passed. Although he'd never needed to use his skills, he'd been trained from an early age for situations like this. If he weren't concerned about hurting Madeline, he could escape her hold. An elbow here. A head slam there. He could easily hook one of her legs out from under her with his and send her tumbling to the floor. But she might impale herself as she fell. So he wouldn't. He'd already violated her trust by deceiving her. He wouldn't add physical injury to his crimes.

"Put the guns on the counter and slide them this way. Grips first," she demanded. "The phone, too."

He signaled with his free hand for Ian and Makos to do as she ordered. Both men looked at him as if he'd lost his mind but after a tense silence complied.

She edged closer to the weapons, towing him along with the knife still at his throat. The sad truth was her strength and bravery impressed him and turned him on. Luckily, he'd donned his pants before coming after her or she and his crew would see exactly how strongly she affected him.

He'd never met a woman like Madeline Spencer. Each time he thought he had her figured out she threw a new and intriguing puzzle piece at him—one that didn't fit his image of her.

Who was this woman who didn't hesitate to defend herself? And what had her ex-fiancé done to disillusion her so about love and to make her so distrustful? It had to be more than merely ending the relationship or finding someone new. And why did the knowledge fill Dominic with rage and a thirst for revenge on her behalf?

She halted a yard from the counter. To use the cell phone she'd have to have at least one hand free. He waited for her to choose between releasing him and putting down the knife, but evidently she came to the same conclusion. "I want to go ashore."

"Then you must allow Ian and Makos to go on deck. We can

be back in Monaco in an hour." That would give him time to convince her to trust and forgive him. He'd had every intention of telling her the truth before making love to her. Each time he'd opened his mouth to do so he had looked into her eyes and considered what he stood to lose. Her sassy, confident smile. Her relaxed yet seductive grace. The easy flow of conversation between a man and a woman who were equals. He'd lived with stiff formality for too many years. She'd given him a taste of what he'd been missing, of what a relationship should be, but what his future marriage would very likely not entail.

Last night when she'd stopped his words with gentle fingers on his lips he'd been weak enough to let desire overrule his conscience, but this morning he hadn't been able to stomach having her call him by the fictitious name. He wanted her crying out his name next time she climaxed.

And there would be a next time. He was more determined than ever to enjoy his last days of freedom in Madeline's company and in her bed. Whatever experience she might believe she lacked as a lover she more than made up for with an earthy sensuality that had brought him pleasure more intense than any he'd ever experienced. He wasn't ready to let her go. Not yet. But soon, unfortunately, he would have to.

She jerked his wrist upward with enough force to get his attention, but not enough to do permanent damage. "How stupid do you think I am? They could sail anywhere."

"You can see the GPS screen from here and know if they sail away from port. You'll have the phone, a pair of handguns and me as your hostage if they head in the wrong direction. And Madeline, my passport is in the cabin. Check it."

Another snort. Another brush of her breasts against his back. Another spark of arousal below his belt. "As if you couldn't fake that."

"Then pull me up on the Internet."

"Gee whiz. I forgot to pack my computer in my beach bag," she drawled sarcastically.

"When we get back to Hôtel Reynard then. I have a laptop in my suite."

"Do you think I'll follow you anywhere after this? And what do you mean 'your suite?' You're staying at Hôtel Reynard?"

"Yes. On the same floor as you, but at the opposite end of the hall in the Royal Suite. We are temporary neighbors. Why else do you think I was waiting for the penthouse elevator the night we met?"

She frowned as she considered that and then growled in anger and shifted on her feet behind him. Each movement rubbed her breasts against his naked back, a distraction he didn't need if he wished to avert disaster.

"Your henchmen can go on deck, but we're locking the door behind them and if they try to come through, I'll shoot because I think you're full of sh—"

"You know how to handle a gun?" Most shooting accidents happened at the hands of the inexperienced and he would prefer to avoid bloodshed. Particularly his.

"My father was a vice cop. I can not only handle a gun, I'm a damned good marksman. He made sure of it."

Ian caught Dominic's attention and tapped his thigh, indicating the smaller weapon Ian kept strapped above his ankle. Dominic signaled the negative and maintained eye contact long enough for the man to understand Dominic would handle the situation. Ian clearly didn't like it, but he accepted Dominic's silent command with a slight nod.

"Pull up anchor and return to port." Dominic's order contradicted every oath his bodyguards had taken. Members of the royal guard had to be willing to die for their country. That meant not leaving one of their leaders with a knife at his throat. But Ian and Makos did as he requested, climbing the ladder and closing the cabin door behind them.

Madeline pulled him toward the hatch and latched it.

"Sit." She shoved him toward the sofa.

Flexing his shoulder, Dominic sat because not fighting would serve his purpose better than asserting his authority or his physical dominance.

Poised on the balls of her feet, Madeline kept the knife at the ready and her eyes fixed on him as she quickly closed the blinds on each window. Smart move. Being unable to see inside the cabin would prevent Ian from trying anything heroic.

To make her feel less threatened Dominic propped his feet on the coffee table, crossed his ankles and leaned back, linking his fingers over his belly. As soon as he did Madeline backed toward the galley and collected the guns.

She handled the firearms comfortably, competently, checking the safeties and the clips of each weapon before shoving the knife back into the drawer. His respect for her climbed another notch. She was smart, resourceful, strong and calm in a crisis. Not to mention sexy as hell.

If a little misguided.

"My passport is in my bag. I'm blond and have a beard in the photo, but you've known me for a week and spent the night in my bed. You should be able to see past facial hair and a temporary dye job."

She kept the width of the room between them. "I don't care about your stupid and probably forged passport. You're still a liar."

Guilty as charged. "I didn't originally intend to conceal my identity, but Madeline, when you looked at me that night by the elevator I saw a woman who desired *me,* not a woman who wanted to land a prince. Do you have any idea how rare that is? It has only happened one other time. With Giselle, my wife."

"Spare me the sob story. I'm sure that was fiction, too."

"Sadly, it is not. I had known Giselle since we were children. We became engaged when I was nineteen and she sixteen."

Her nose wrinkled in distaste. "That's positively feudal."

He shrugged, but didn't waste time trying to explain a bridal selection process he knew she would neither like nor understand. "I agree. She was too young. That is why I insisted we postpone the marriage until I graduated from the university. And then as I told you in the café, she died two years into our marriage along with our first child."

"I don't want to hear it."

He ignored her words and kept talking to keep her calm and to get her to let down her guard. "My country is raw and largely untamed due to the royal advisory council's fear of change."

She rolled her eyes. "Uh-huh."

"It is believed that Montagnarde was once a massive volcano, but sixty million years ago the ocean breached the walls and extinguished the fire. There are three islands now surrounding an inland sea of crystal clear water."

"What a great imagination. You should write a book."

He smiled at her acid tone. She didn't believe him. Would she, like so many others, become deferential, obsequious and more interested in what his wealth and power could do for her once she accepted his identity? Undoubtedly. And when she did he was certain his fascination with her would end. "My youngest sister is writing a history of the islands. I have three sisters. Danielle, Yvette and Brigitte.

"Each generation of monarchs must have an agenda. My great-grandfather's was to protect our borders from outsiders and pests which might devastate our crops or wildlife. My grandfather focused on building a first-class transportation system within and around the islands, and my father on exporting our products. I am determined to introduce the world to the beauty of Montagnarde. Like Monaco, we should maximize our tourist potential. That is why I focused my degree and the past ten years' study on tourism. I intend to implement change and put my country on the map."

"So you admit 'your country' isn't on the map." More sarcasm.

"In terms of global recognition, not yet. But our wines, olive oils and organic produce are beginning to find success in foreign markets. As for our tourism development potential, we have mountains suited to skiing or climbing, depending on the season, blue seas perfect for sailing, sport fishing or surfing, underwater caverns to explore and hot mineral springs for rejuvenation. The natural reefs off our shores put the man-made ones in Monaco to shame and the species of fish and marine life are incredible."

The urgency to share the beauty of his country with her was unexpected and unwelcome, not to mention impossible. "The emeralds mined in Montagnarde are almost as lovely as your eyes, Madeline."

She snorted. "Save your breath. I am *so* over your flattery and so over you."

Frustration rose within him. He had power and wealth at his fingertips and yet the one thing he wished for he couldn't have. He wished for more time with Madeline. But time was a luxury he did not have….

Unless he could turn this disaster to his advantage.

A gurgle of disgust erupted from Madeline's throat. "You are really something."

"So you told me last night. I believe *magnificent* is the word you used."

She wanted to smack that confident smirk off Damon's face. A shocking fact, since she'd never been one prone to violence. Her cheeks burned hot. She'd been a fool for swallowing his garbage the way she had Mike's. Just how stupid was she to let two handsome faces override her common sense?

"Keep it up, bucko, and I might just shoot you for the fun of it. I don't like being made a fool of."

"Is that what your ex did? Made you look foolish?"

She very deliberately released the safety on the gun. "It's not smart to piss off an armed lady."

Damon held up his hands as if in surrender. "Then I will tell you more about my homeland instead." He lowered his arms and linked his fingers over his navel. She could not believe she had nibbled her way down that lying rat's goodie trail last night.

Worse, the proof of Damon's deceit had been right in front of her. Only she'd failed to see the signs because the lights had been out. Sort of like her relationship with Mike. She'd only seen what she wanted to see until he'd forced her to acknowledge the truth.

She hated feeling stupid. Clueless. Duped.

"Each of the islands of Montagnarde has one or more glacial lakes with water pure enough to bottle. The streams and rivers are a fisherman's paradise. Like New Zealand, we have no poisonous snakes or spiders."

Blah. Blah. Blah. She focused on the GPS screen and tried to tune out his words. Whatever he said would be more lies anyway. She could hear the men above them moving about and raising the sails.

Trapped on a yacht with a trio of lunatics. What had she done to deserve this? And would she live to tell the tale?

Yes, dammit, you will. Your mother's depending on you.

"My country was discovered in the 1700s by the Comte de Rossi, a Frenchman searching for a shorter route to the spices of India," he continued. "His ships veered off course in a storm. He landed on the main island searching for food and to make repairs. He decided to stay and explore."

"Right. And the natives just let the French drop anchor and take over?"

"Initially, the islands' inhabitants were bribed with the luxuries on board the ships, but sadly, within the first year the majority of them were decimated by European diseases—also on board de Rossi's ships. The Comte, owner of the fleet, declared himself king and named the islands Montagnarde for the peaks that pierced the clouds. During his lifetime he selectively allowed his countrymen and the finest craftsmen to immigrate, and it is said his advisors kidnapped the most beautiful woman in all of France to be his bride and queen."

Until he uttered the last part his tall tale had *almost* sounded plausible. Her mouth dried. "You'd better not be thinking along the same lines."

"I regret that our affair must end when I leave Monaco."

"In case you missed the bulletin, our affair is already over." Her stomach growled. She glanced at the coffeepot and inhaled the aroma of the strong brew. Her racing heart didn't need the caffeine jolt, but she did need something in her empty stomach to counteract the light-headedness caused by an adrenaline rush combined with not replacing the large number of calories she'd burned off in the past twelve hours.

Naked and entwined with the dishonest snake.

With a gun in her right hand she found a mug with her left and mounded a diet-wrecking amount of sugar inside, and then she poured a stream of coffee on top and swished it around to mix it. She didn't risk taking her eyes off Dominic long enough to search for a spoon or cream. She sipped the syrupy brew. *Eeew.*

"There are pastries in the cabinet to your left and eggs, sausage, fruit and cheese in the refrigerator."

His words made her salivate, but blocking her view of her captive to search the fridge was out of the question. "You'd love it if I'd drop my guard, wouldn't you?"

"I would enjoy breakfast more. We worked up quite an appetite last night."

Her body flushed all over. "Jerk."

She opened the cabinet, found the croissants and hurled one at him with enough force to break a window had it been a rock.

He snagged it out of the air. "Thank you. I am fond of Ian's coffee, as well."

She almost flung her mug at him. Instead she extracted another from the cabinet, filled it and shoved it to the far end of the bar. He was out of luck if he wanted cream or sugar.

He rose and slowly approached. "You don't need the gun, Madeline."

She cursed him, using the one four-letter word she *never* used and he grinned.

"I believe you did that last night. Three times. And with extremely satisfying results."

She gaped. Did the man have an ounce of sense? She had a loaded gun in her hand and he insisted on provoking her.

He moved around the end of the bar. Good God, she didn't want to shoot him. She didn't take lives. She saved them. And until he'd betrayed her she'd liked him. Maybe she could just maim him. But where? She considered her artery-avoiding options. "Don't even think about it."

He stopped his advance and leaned his hip against the counter.

"I can think of nothing but the softness of your skin. Your scent. Your taste. That voracious mouth. The slick clench of your body as you drove me out of my mind. I have never desired a woman as I do you, Madeline. And we could be rediscovering that passion at this moment if you would put the gun down."

Damn him and his low-pitched seductive voice. Arousal tumbled through her. How was that possible in this situation? She briefly closed her eyes—no more than a blink—as the images of last night inundated her, and in that split second Damon lunged forward. His long fingers latched around her wrist. He shoved her gun hand toward the ceiling and slammed his body into hers, backing her against the refrigerator door and forcing the breath from her lungs. The gun exploded with a deafening sound and bits of ceiling rained down.

She struggled, but Damon had her pinned like an insect on a collector's board with his broad chest, his muscular hips and rock-hard thighs grinding against hers.

"Release the gun, Madeline," he ordered calmly.

The hatch door rattled viciously.

"Release the gun," he repeated this time with his warm breath and prickly morning stubble against her jaw. "I promise you are in no danger."

There was nothing remotely sexy about wrestling for a gun, and yet there wasn't an inch of him she couldn't feel imprinted on her skin. Her traitorous brain remembered being this close to him just hours ago with nothing but a thin sheen of sweat between them. How dare her body betray her at this moment. She stiffened her softening muscles.

"As if I'd believe anything you say," she muttered and tried to bow her spine to earn some breathing room.

"You have no choice." There was a hard, commanding edge to his voice that hadn't been there before.

Her hand started to go numb from the pressure he exerted on her radial nerve. Her grip loosened at the same time as the hatch splintered open. Over Damon's shoulder she saw Ian charge in, leading with a small pistol.

"Stand down," Damon called out. His big body blocked hers from his henchmen. He held up his hand, displaying the weapon he'd taken from her.

The other gun lay on the counter out of reach.

Damn. Damn. Damn. She'd let her guard down. Had her father been alive he would have been disappointed in her. Determined she would never be a victim of the kind of crimes he investigated, he'd drilled self-defense techniques into her once a week from the day he'd moved out.

"Ian, Makos, retrieve your weapons. Mademoiselle Spencer will be joining me in the captain's cabin."

"In your dreams, *prince*." She practically spat his fake title.

"Give us a few moments and then we would like breakfast." He grasped each of her arms and then lifted his weight and yanked her forward before transferring her wrists to one big hand behind her back. His long fingers compressed like a vise.

"Don't make me tie you up," he murmured in her ear. "Although we might enjoy that another time."

"Bite me."

"I would be more than happy to in the privacy of our cabin." He turned her and steered her toward the cabin. Try as she might she could not wriggle free. Man, the guy was strong. And then he closed the door and locked it behind them. Damon released her.

She hustled to the far side of the room, scanning the surfaces for weapons and finding none. Not even a vase to crack over his head. But even if she incapacitated him she'd still have to deal with the two armed thugs in the other room.

He reached into his luggage, withdrew something and tossed it onto the bed. His passport fell open to the picture and her breath caught. As handsome as Damon was as a brunette, he was drop-dead gorgeous as a blond with his hair slicked back to reveal his amazing bone structure and those pale blue eyes.

She inched closer and snatched up the booklet. It named him as Prince Dominic Andreas Rossi de Montagnarde. Hair: blond. Eyes: blue. Height: six feet three inches. She did the math and came up with his age: thirty-five. She flipped through the pages and read stamped ports of entry from across the globe.

But the "passport" was a fake. It had to be. Princes didn't pretend to be tour guides. They traveled with an entourage of toadying staff, and they didn't hang out with commoners like her. She knew that much from *CNN*.

Was Damon some sort of charlatan who connived his way around the globe with a false title? With his looks, charm and sexual prowess he could swindle big-time. But he should focus on women with money. Maybe he thought she was loaded because she'd told him she'd be in Monaco an entire month.

"Recognize me now?" he asked.

"No. And it doesn't matter anyway because once we dock I don't ever want to see you again unless it's to ID you in a police lineup." She flung the documentation back onto the tangled sheets and tried not to recall how the linens had become so mussed.

"I am very sorry to hear that. Because I have not had my fill of you, Madeline. I find your company quite refreshing."

"Too bad." She paced the length of the cabin. "Okay, here's the deal. Put me ashore and I'll forget this ever happened. I won't report you or your thugs."

Not exactly the truth, but—

"Good try, but no." Damon sat on the bed, stretched his legs out before him and leaned back against the headboard, looking as comfortable as he had in the middle of last night when he'd sat in the same spot and watched her shower through the open bathroom door. The memory of how he'd taken the towel from her and lapped the water from her skin afterward shortened her breath and tightened her nipples. She turned her back and stared out the narrow window. Better that than look at his naked chest and remember what an idiot she'd been last night and what an idiot she was being right now by getting distracted by sex.

Wasn't it just her luck that the best lover she'd ever had was a step lower on the slug meter than Mike? Her ex might have been a liar and a cheat, but as far as she knew he'd never broken the law or stooped to kidnapping.

Twenty tense, silent minutes later a knock on the door brought Damon to his feet. He let Ian and breakfast in and then relocked the door after the man left. Food was the last thing she wanted, but if she had to swim or run for it then she'd need whatever fuel she could get. She inched toward the tray while Damon pulled on a blue shirt with a gold crest on the pocket and traded his wrinkled pants for clean briefs and a pressed pair of khakis. He buttoned the shirt and tucked it in, adding a leather belt, and then he stepped into rubber-soled boat shoes. As a final touch he raked his hair back off his forehead with his fingers, exposing his aristocratic bone structure. In that getup he looked like one of the rich and famous. Very "yacht club" and a far cry from her tour guide-lover-kidnapper.

"You realize you have threatened the life of a monarch?" Damon asked casually as he spread cherry preserves on a croissant.

How long was he going to persist in that fairy-tale garbage? Grabbing a pastry with one hand, she flipped him a rude gesture with the other. She bit through the flaky crust and into the moist croissant, chewed, swallowed with inelegant haste until she'd consumed most of her breakfast-fuel supply.

He finished his with less speed, poured a cup of coffee and sipped. "The offense is punishable by imprisonment or death in my country."

She nearly choked on her last bite of pastry and then gulped down the formerly butter-rich now tasteless wad. It hit her stomach like lead. His threat wasn't funny. She'd been worried before, but this ratcheted up the tension in her muscles another ten notches. What exactly was she dealing with here? Because she didn't believe for one second that he actually was royalty.

She eyed the coffee carafe and considered whacking him with it. Did it have enough weight to knock him out? And then what would she do? "We're not in your country."

"The Monaco authorities will be even less lenient."

Other than a sick churning in her stomach she had no answer for that. She wished she'd used Ian's cell phone to call Candace and Amelia and ask them to send the harbor police or whatever they were called.

Who would look after her mother if Madeline ended up not making it back to Charlotte? May Spencer wasn't in fragile health yet, but she was seventy-eight. She didn't travel well and flying made her seriously ill. Would she be able to handle a trip overseas to search for her missing daughter?

Don't think like that. Damon hasn't hurt you. In fact, he stepped between you and the goons' guns twice. Surely if he intended to harm you he wouldn't have?

Or maybe she was worth more alive than dead.

"What do you want from me? I don't have any money. My father is dead and my mother lives on a cop's and a retired teacher's pensions. Trust me, that's a pittance. And I hear the U.S. doesn't negotiate with terrorists."

"I am neither a terrorist nor a kidnapper. I merely wish to continue our…assignations."

Her mouth dropped open. Was he nuts? *Of course he is. He thinks he's a freaking prince.* "You want to remain my tour guide?"

"I would prefer to be your companion and your lover for the remainder of your vacation and mine."

The man had balls of steel and a pea-size brain. "I don't do forced sex."

His bearing snapped military straight and his aristocratic nose lifted. He had the arrogance thing down pat, and he even looked like royalty for a minute there. "I am neither a rapist nor an extortionist. When you return to my bed, Madeline, it will be because you desire me as much as you did last night."

How ungentlemanly of him to mention her enthusiasm. "Not going to happen."

"Would you care to place a wager on that?" One corner of his mouth slanted upward.

Foot stomping overhead followed by the boat's engine rumbling to life preempted her scathing reply—which was a good thing since she couldn't think of one. She moved back to the window and saw the port of Monaco in the distance— swimmable distance if she could get out of this cabin and past the thugs who sounded like elephants overhead. She eyed the skylight in the ceiling, but there was no way she could reach it let alone get through it before Damon could grab her legs.

"We have reached the marina," Damon stated.

Fifteen minutes later the sound of voices—more than had occupied the dock when they'd left—filtered through the closed windows. Damon looked outside and cursed. "Paparazzi. Along with the Sûreté Publique. Ian must have called for assistance."

The police? Thank God. She pressed a palm to her chest.

He caught her shoulders and her gaze. "You will do exactly as I say when we disembark. I would not like to see you inadvertently injured."

"And if I don't?"

"I will press charges."

Jeez, how long was he going to play this gig?

All she had to do was agree. She'd be screaming for help the second she got outside, but he didn't need to know that. She'd report him to the authorities, and she'd tell Vincent Reynard and have the imposter kicked out of the hotel—maybe even banned from all of Reynard's hotels worldwide. Maybe the Monaco Sûreté Publique would haul Damon off in handcuffs. After the scare he'd given her she'd enjoy watching that.

"Okay. I'll do what you say." The lie didn't even make her twitch.

The boat bumped against the dock. Heavy footsteps immediately boarded, rocking the craft.

"Follow my lead and do not say anything to incriminate yourself."

Incriminate herself? That was a riot coming from a con man.

Keeping her behind him Damon opened the cabin door and rattled off something in French. Madeline ducked under his arm, intending to sprint for the hatch, but she skidded to a halt at the sight of the overcrowded galley.

Police. Six of them. With weapons drawn. They fired off commands—commands she couldn't understand and moved toward her in a threatening manner. She backed into Damon.

"English please." Damon's hands encircled her waist and

then he shifted her to his side and draped an arm across her shoulders as if they were friends. Or lovers. "Mademoiselle Spencer does not speak French. And the weapons are unnecessary. She is unarmed."

"You are under arrest, mademoiselle, for assaulting Prince Dominic," one of the officers said.

She gaped. "Me? What about him and his henchmen? They kidnapped me!"

Two of the men reached for her but Damon stopped them with an outstretched and upraised hand. "I apologize for wasting your time, officers. My bodyguards misunderstood the nature of our—" he paused to stare intently into Madeline's eyes "—love play."

He compounded that lie by kissing the tip of her nose.

Her cheeks caught fire over the insinuation while confusion tumbled through her brain. "That's not what hap—"

"Madeline." Damon cupped her shoulders and gave her a gentle shake. "The game is over. You do not want the police to arrest you. Do you?"

She looked from the officers to Damon and back again. The cops had handcuffs, guns and attitude. Enough testosterone crackled in the air to fill a Super Bowl team's locker room. She had encountered hundreds of law enforcement officers through her father and in the E.R.—enough to recognize the real deal when she saw it. These guys weren't pretending. And apparently Damon—*Dominic*—whatever he called himself, wasn't, either.

Her stomach lurched. She gulped back the breakfast rising in her throat and turned to the nearest uniformed man, a fox-faced guy about her age. "He's really a prince?"

The man blinked in surprise. *"Oui,* mademoiselle. Prince Dominic is a frequent and welcome visitor to Monaco."

Uh-oh.

"If you would give us a moment to gather our belongings," Damon said in more of an order than request, "I would be most grateful if you could assist us through the paparazzi outside."

A man whose name tag read Inspector Rousseau said, "*Certainement,* Your Highness. We are happy to be of service."

Numbly, Madeline allowed Damon to steer her back into the cabin. She closed her eyes and locked her jaws on a groan.

Oh, spit. She really had assaulted a member of royalty.

This was *so* not how she'd planned to spend her vacation.

Five

"I guess 'Oops, I'm sorry' won't cut it?" Madeline asked Dam—Prince Dominic in a barely audible voice. She glanced over her shoulder at the officers watching diligently from outside the open door.

"That depends on whether or not you agree to my terms," he replied as quietly.

Her stomach knotted. "Continue the, uh…relationship?"

Dominic nodded once—sharply—with his gaze drilling into hers. Funny how regal he looked all of a sudden. "And you will keep details of our affair private. I have no wish to read about my Monaco mistress in the tabloids."

The Prince's Monaco Mistress. She could see the headlines now. Ugh. She'd never wanted to be famous—certainly not famous for stupidity. Being humiliated by Mike in her small corner of the world had been more than enough exposure, thanks very much.

Spending time with a man who'd lied to her and tricked her into bed under false pretenses ranked low on her to-do list. But it beat incarceration. She knew nothing about Monaco law except the country had an extremely low tolerance for crime. There were cameras on every street corner as a deterrent. Even if she could convince a judge or whoever was in charge of the legal system here to understand her side, she couldn't afford to worry her mother, and she'd prefer not to ruin Candace's wedding with a scandal. And then there was the likelihood that getting arrested would probably jeopardize her job.

"Fine," she bit out ungraciously. "But remember, you are not the prince of me. I'm not doing anything illegal, immoral or disgusting no matter what you threaten."

His lips twitched. "Duly noted. You have two minutes to make whatever adjustments you wish to your appearance before we face the paparazzi."

She ducked into the bathroom and quickly cleaned up, then returned to the bedroom.

"Put on your hat and sunglasses," Da—Dominic ordered. The new name would take some getting used to.

Madeline complied. The last thing she wanted her mother or her coworkers at the hospital to see was her face on *CNN* or *Entertainment Tonight*.

"Your hair is easily recognizable. You might wish to conceal it beneath your hat."

She twisted it into a rope and shoved it beneath the cap.

"Once we exit the yacht keep your head down and do not answer any questions no matter how provocative."

Once they had their bags packed he took hers from her and turned back to address the police through the open door. "Officers, once again I apologize for the misunderstanding.

Should you require it, I will be more than happy to come down
to the station and make an official report after I return Mademoiselle Spencer to the hotel."

"That will not be necessary, Your Highness," Rousseau said.

The youngest officer offered to carry their bags. Dominic
handed them off and strode toward the hatch.

Where had her sexy, laid-back tour guide gone? The man
in front of her stood straight, tall and regal as he followed half
of the officers from the cabin.

How could he follow and still give the impression of leading?

He paused at the top of the ladder and turned to help
Madeline ascend. The wall of voices and the whir of cameras
slammed her as soon as her head cleared the cabin. She pulled
down the bill of her cap. From the dock, dozens of camera-
toting reporters shouted questions in a variety of languages.
Dominic ignored them.

No, *ignore* wasn't quite the correct word. He acted as if he
didn't see or hear them, as if they didn't exist.

"Head down. Let's go," he said into her ear and then he
grabbed her elbow and half led, half dragged her over the
planks in the wake of three officers who cleared a path. Ian
and Makos followed with two other officers behind them.
One remained on the boat—to guard it, she presumed. Or to
write up a damage report. She winced. No telling how much
paying for those repairs was going to set her back.

The crush of sweaty, smelly bodies jostling to get a picture
of Dominic nearly overwhelmed her. The only other time
she'd seen something even remotely close to this was when
Vincent, Candace's fiancé, had been brought to the E.R. after
being badly burned last year at a NASCAR race. The press
had crowded into the lobby of the E.R. and security had struggled to keep them out.

A white Mercedes limo waited by the curb. An attendant opened the door as they approached. Dominic urged her to enter first. He quickly followed, choosing the seat directly across from hers. The door closed and silence and blessedly cool air-conditioned air enfolded them. The trunk thumped shut, presumably on their bags.

She looked at the milling crowd outside the tinted windows. The police kept them away from the car. "You live like this?"

"Yes. Now do you understand the need for a disguise?"

She could see how it might appeal, but still— "You should have told me who you were before we slept together."

He nodded acknowledgment. "Agreed."

She waited for him to make excuses. He didn't.

The driver climbed in. Ian joined him in the front seat. Their doors shut with a quiet *thunk* that shouted expensive car.

"The hotel, Your Highness?" the driver asked through an open black glass panel between the front and back seats.

"Yes." The glass rose and the car moved forward.

Angry and confused, Madeline shifted uneasily on the leather seat and then ripped off her sunglasses. "What game were you playing? Slumming with the commoner who didn't have the sense to know who you were? Were you laughing at my ignorance the entire time?"

"I have never considered you ignorant. Nor did I laugh at you. I enjoyed your lack of pretense. Revealing my identity would have changed that."

"You think I'm going to suck up to you now?"

He studied her appraisingly from behind dark lenses. "In my experience I find it likely."

"In your dreams, bucko." And then she recalled the protocol lessons from Candace's future sister-in-law. *Never address royalty by their first names.* "Do you expect me to call you 'Your Highness?' Because I have kissed your butt—literally. I'll be damned if I'll start bowing and scraping—"

His low chuckle winded her. "I would prefer you did not."

"Okay then. Now what? I can't imagine our outings will be any fun if we have to contend with that." She nodded toward the crowd they'd left behind—the one now scurrying along the sidewalk like a fat millipede trying to keep up with them. She couldn't imagine the dates would be fun period since she'd be participating under duress.

"We will have to be more resourceful."

"Where's your entourage? Every bigwig I've seen on TV has one."

"I left them behind. This was supposed to be a quiet, incognito vacation. Ian will arrange for additional security."

At least with security men around there wouldn't be any more intimate encounters. "How long before you accept my apology and let me off the hook?"

"Not until I tire of your company." He leaned forward and splayed his palms across her knees and lower thighs. Heat shot upward from the points of contact. "And, Madeline, I don't think that will happen anytime soon."

The sensual promise in his voice and his touch melted her anger frighteningly fast. She abruptly shifted her legs out of reach and struggled to rally her flagging ire. "Just don't expect me to sleep with you again."

He sat back and looked down his aristocratic nose at her. "You have issued that challenge once already. Repeating it only makes me more determined to prove you wrong."

"We will have lunch in my suite," Dominic announced as they exited the elevator on the hotel's penthouse floor.

"I don't think so." Eager to escape, Madeline turned in the opposite direction and marched toward her suite.

He followed, along with his bodyguards. "I insist."

She stopped outside her door and glared at him. "Insist all you want. But the answer's still no. You don't own every minute of my time. That wasn't part of our deal. I want a shower and a few hours away from you. In case you haven't noticed, I'm still ticked off."

She swiped her electronic key card. The latch whirred and the green light winked. She extended her hand. "Give me my bag."

"Give me your passport."

"Are you nuts?" *Isn't that becoming a familiar refrain?*

"I will not allow you to flee Monaco and escape fulfilling your end of our bargain."

The idea appealed. Immensely. "I can't leave. I have a friend's wedding to help plan and to be in. *I* would never screw someone who trusted me."

From the tightening of his lips she guessed he hadn't missed her implication that he had. "Regardless, I will take your passport as insurance."

The door opened and Amelia stood in the threshold, her hazel eyes cautious as she took in the foursome in the hall. "Is everything okay?"

"No, everything is not okay," Madeline informed her.

Dominic bowed slightly, turning on the charm and flashing a high wattage smile. The action made Amelia's cheeks flush and Madeline seethe. "*Bonjour,* mademoiselle."

"Um, hi." Amelia's gaze flicked back and forth between the men and Madeline.

Madeline grimaced. She'd have to make introductions even though she'd prefer to keep starry-eyed Amelia away from His

Royal Pain in the Butt. Amelia was waiting for a prince to sweep her off her feet. But not this prince.

"Amelia Lambert, my friend, suitemate and coworker. This is Da—Dominic— How in the hell am I supposed to introduce you?"

Dominic's eyes twinkled as if she'd asked a loaded question, and Madeline's pulse tripped.

Stop that. You are immune to him now.

He offered his hand to Amelia. "Dominic Rossi."

Madeline waited, but he didn't offer his title. "He's a freaking prince. And my former tour guide."

Amelia snatched her hand from Dominic's. "Excuse me?"

"The lying snake in the grass omitted telling me he's royalty. The big guys are his bodyguards, Ian and Makos." She jerked a thumb toward the lurking men.

Amelia blinked uncertainly. "Um, nice to meet you?"

"I'll explain later. Just let me in."

Amelia stepped back, opening the door wider. Madeline jerked her bag from Dominic's hand and squeezed past her friend. Dominic, damn him, followed. Ian and Makos remained in the hall like big totem poles flanking the door.

"Your passport, Madeline," Dominic reminded her. "Or I can call the Sûreté Publique."

"Go to he—"

"Why does he need to call the police?" Amelia interrupted. "Did something happen?"

Madeline fought the urge to squirm and glared at Dominic. "We had a misunderstanding, which, of course, was entirely *his* fault."

"It is hardly my fault you chose not to believe the truth," he replied in an infuriatingly calm voice.

"Since you'd been so honest up until that point?" she drawled sarcastically.

He had the decency to flush.

"The prince of what?" Amelia, bless her peacemaking heart, interrupted again.

"Montagnarde," Dominic replied, directing another one of his ligament-loosening smiles her friend's way.

"Really?" she whispered in an awestruck voice.

Surprised, Madeline stared. "You've heard of the place?"

"Absolutely. It's southwest of Hawaii. All the burn unit nurses want to go there—if we ever win the lottery, that is. The queen's books about an adventurous dragon are immensely popular with the children on the floor."

Madeline's gaze bounced from Dominic to Amelia and back. Was she the only one without a clue about him or his homeland? "You said your sister was the author."

"Brigitte is writing a history of the islands, but my mother writes children's books. They're the stories she told my sisters and me when we were young."

She did not want to picture him as a boy curled up in his mother's lap for a bedtime story. He'd probably been disgustingly cute then, too.

Amelia frowned and narrowed her eyes on Dominic. "Forgive my impertinence, Your uh, Highness? But I thought you were a blond and you…" She pointed at her jawline.

"Dominic, please." He pulled out his wallet, extracted a business card and offered it to Amelia. "I was incognito until Madeline broke my cover. E-mail the hospital address to me and I will have Mama send a box of autographed books to your hospital. If you would like, you may include the first names of the children currently residing on the floor so she can personalize them."

Wide-eyed, Amelia clutched the card to her chest. "I'll do that as soon as I get back to Charlotte. Thank you."

Madeline clenched her teeth. She did not want him doing nice stuff. She'd rather remember him as the sneaky, lying bastard forcing his company on her.

And he hadn't given *her* a card. Not that she wanted one. Nope. She'd be happy if she never laid eyes on him, his card or his henchmen ever again.

His blue gaze caught Madeline's. "Perhaps Mademoiselle Lambert would like to join us for lunch in my suite."

The moment she saw the pleasure bloom in Amelia's face, Madeline knew she should have killed Da—Dominic while she had the chance. The conniving opportunist had set the trap so smoothly she hadn't seen it and she'd stepped right into it. If she refused to eat with him now Amelia would be crushed.

Madeline flipped him a rude hand gesture behind her friend's back.

His smile turned wicked. "I'll take that as a yes."

Grrr. "May I see you in my room for a moment?"

"My pleasure."

"You wish." She turned her back on Amelia's dreamy sigh, stomped into her bedroom, tapped her toe impatiently until he crossed the threshold and then shut the door behind him with a restrained click. Slamming it would have been much more satisfying. She settled for heaving her overnight bag onto the bed and then planting her fists on her hips.

"Leave Amelia out of this."

"Your friend is charming."

"And off-limits to you." If the lift of his eyebrow was any indication, her tone had sounded a tad too possessive. Or protective. Or bitchy. Probably all three. "Should I expect more underhanded maneuvering from you?"

"Only if you make it necessary. I am usually quite straight-forward in my desires. And at the moment I desire your company...and you, Madeline."

Her pulse tripped over the raspy edge of his voice and her body heated at the memory of exactly what fulfilling his desires had entailed. He hadn't neglected one single inch of *her* body last night while taking care of *his* needs.

"Can't say the same about yours and you," she lied with only a pinch of discomfort.

His smile turned predatory. "Another challenge?"

She almost snarled, but settled for a glare.

He extended his hand. "Your passport, please."

"What if I want to cross the border on a sightseeing trip?"

"You will be with me, and I will have your passport. Tomorrow morning we'll go to the Rainier III Shooting Range. I wish to see how good you are with a weapon."

She ungraciously dug her passport out of the dresser drawer, slapped it into his hand and then studied her nails. "I might be busy."

"You're afraid I'm a better marksman?" He slipped the booklet into his pants pocket.

"Don't try reverse psychology on me. It won't work."

He moved closer. The dresser behind her prevented her escape. He lifted his hand and dragged a fingertip along the skin fluttering wildly over her carotid artery. "Would you prefer I stroke your erogenous zones instead? As I recall, that made you quite amenable last night."

She cursed her weakening knees and the revealing goose bumps marching across her skin. Last night his caresses had turned her mind and body to mush. She would have agreed to practically anything he asked.

But that was then. Now she knew he was the kind of guy

who'd lie his way into a woman's bed. She clenched her teeth, jerked her head out of reach and folded her arms across her tattletale breasts. She ought to plant a knee in his crotch.

He must have read her mind because he lowered his hand and stepped back. "I will expect you and Mademoiselle Lambert in my suite in an hour. And Madeline, do not disappoint me."

A stranger opened the door. A gorgeous, blond-haired, blue-eyed, freshly shaven stranger expensively attired in a dove-gray suit and a stark white open-collared shirt.

Dominic. Madeline's mouth dried and her heart stuttered. She'd recognize that incredible bone structure anywhere. He'd been handsome as a brunette, but now... *Wow*. He'd brushed his hair back from his forehead, setting off his pale blue eyes and tanned skin.

But his phenomenal looks didn't matter. She had a zero tolerance policy for liars. "You have a hairdresser at your beck and call?"

Her waspish question didn't faze him. "Hôtel Reynard is quite accommodating. Come in, mesdemoiselles."

The layout and opulence of his suite resembled the one she shared with Amelia, Candace and Stacy, but whereas theirs was light and airy, his was decorated in jewel-tone fabrics and darker woods. The dining room table had been set with enough silver, crystal and china to buckle the legs of a less substantial piece of furniture. Afternoon sunlight streamed through the floor-to-ceiling windows overlooking the Mediterranean, making the wine and water goblets sparkle like diamonds scattered across the ivory linen tablecloth.

Rich. Formal. Elegant. Dominic's world. She was only a visitor—and a reluctant one at that. Better not forget it.

She felt the weight of Dominic's gaze on her as she studied

the setup. He believed his having loads of money would impress her. But he was wrong. She worked with dozens of consulting doctors and surgeons through the E.R. Some were incredibly wealthy, certainly not in Dominic's heir-to-the-kingdom league, but a money surplus didn't keep them from being jackasses. A seven- or eight-figure net worth meant nothing if no one liked, respected or trusted you.

Self-satisfaction was more important than mucho bucks any day. She wanted to work where she could help the largest number of people and maybe even catch a few lost souls before they slipped through the bureaucratic health-care cracks. A county hospital provided the best venue. And when her head hit the pillow each night she could rest easy knowing she'd made a difference that day. The way her father had as a cop. The way her mother had as an inner-city schoolteacher.

She glanced at her friend. Amelia seemed a little ill at ease around *Prince* Dominic. Or maybe it was the four waiters lined up like a firing squad on the far wall or the stone-faced Ian over in the corner making her uneasy.

"He doesn't like me much, does he?" Madeline asked sotto voce so the bodyguard in question wouldn't overhear.

"Would you expect otherwise? You threatened to slit my throat," Dominic replied in an equally quiet tone—but not so quiet she missed the amusement tingeing his voice.

"Madeline!" Amelia squeaked.

Madeline winced. She'd escaped telling Amelia what happened by ducking into the shower and dawdling over dressing for lunch. The extra care she'd taken with her appearance had absolutely nothing to do with impressing Dominic. She didn't care if he liked her slim-fitting lime-green sundress or her strappy sandals. She'd chosen this outfit because it complemented her eyes and showed off her hard-earned shape.

Right now she needed the confidence booster of looking good because she felt stupid. Not an emotion she enjoyed or one she experienced often, thank goodness. She had a reputation at work for thinking fast on her feet and being good in a crisis. That would be worthless if this debacle slipped out. Talk about jumping to erroneous conclusions… She'd taken a dive into the Mariana Trench.

"Rest assured, Mademoiselle Lambert, Madeline had reason to question her safety. But that is something we shall not discuss around outsiders." Dominic indicated the waiters with a slight inclination of his head.

His defense surprised Madeline as did the reminder that others would be interested in his life.

"Please be seated." He touched his hand to the base of Madeline's spine and sparks skipped up her vertebrae like stones skimming across a pond's surface. Her breath hitched. She didn't look at him as she crossed the long room to the lavishly laid table.

Frankly, the entire episode, or rather her lack of perception, was embarrassing. How could she have believed him to be a simple tour guide? From his fluency with languages to his expensive clothing, his regal bearing and complete acceptance of the waiters rushing forward to pull back their chairs, everything about Dominic screamed wealth and privilege.

Dominic stood behind the seat at the head of the table, waiting for the staff to seat Madeline on his right and Amelia on his left. Once the women were settled he sat and commenced a wine tasting ritual that launched a meal more elaborate than any Madeline had ever experienced. Each mouthwatering course arrived hot and fresh from the kitchen, and then finally, what seemed like forever later, the waiters placed dessert in front of them. Dominic dismissed the servers. Only Ian remained in watchful silence.

Madeline stared at the confection in front of her. She didn't even want to think about how many calories she'd consumed or how many extra hours she'd have to spend in the hotel gym to make up for this meal. But that didn't stop her from sampling the warm chocolate tart topped with Bavarian cream mousse. She'd never tasted anything as rich, decadent and delicious. Her mouth practically had an orgasm. Her eyes closed and a moan sneaked past her lips.

Embarrassed, she pressed her napkin to her lips and peeked at Dominic only to find his attention riveted on her face. His pupils dilated and his intense gaze shifted to her mouth. His lips parted slightly and he moistened them with his tongue. A slowly indrawn breath expanded his chest.

The raw passion in his eyes torched her body like dry kindling. Memories of his lovemaking licked through her. His touch. His taste. His incredible heat. The powerful surge of his body into hers.

Her skin flushed and dampened. The fabric of her dress abraded her suddenly sensitive breasts and desire pooled and pulsed in her pelvis.

So much for pretending indifference or forgetting even one second of last night. If a single desire-laden glance from his bedroom blue eyes could bring it all rushing back, then staying out of his bed wasn't going to be nearly as easy as she'd hoped.

Well, dammit, she'd just have to try harder. Failure wasn't an option.

She makes the same sound when she climaxes.

Madeline's moan hit Dominic like a sucker punch. Memories of their passionate night erupted inside him with the force of a volcano. Desire coursed through his veins like streams of molten lava. He instantly recalled the slick, tight heat of her body, the scrape of her nails on his back as she arched beneath him and the band of her legs around his hips urging him deeper.

She scowled at him and flicked back her hair. Remembering the sweep of her soft curls across his belly as she took him into her hot, wet mouth made him shudder. From the toes curled in his shoes to his clenched jaw, each of his muscles contracted. Sweat beaded on his upper lip.

He had spent the past two hours waiting for Madeline to become cloying, obsequious and more interested in what his wealth and power could do for her. As soon as she did he was certain his fascination with her would end.

The elaborate luncheon had been but a small sample of the luxuries he could shower upon her now that his identity had been revealed. But instead of using her position as his lover as leverage, other than an occasional unsuccessful attempt to derail the conversational path he'd chosen, she'd been unusually reticent.

She'd barely contributed to the discussion about the sights and clubs she and her suitemates had already visited or the upcoming wedding—the reason for her presence in Monaco. Her friend had been more forthcoming, but Amelia's comments had only led to more questions about the puzzling Madeline Spencer.

Finally, Amelia pushed her dessert plate away.

"You enjoyed lunch?" He hoped his impatience didn't show.

"Yes. Thank you so much for including me, Your Highness."

"Dominic. And it was my pleasure."

Her cheeks flushed. "Dominic."

He should be polite and linger over coffee, but he had lost

ground to recover and a limited time in which to do so. He stood. "Ian, please escort Mademoiselle Lambert to her suite."

Madeline shoved back her chair and rose. "I'm going, too."

Dominic caught her wrist and held firmly when she tried to pull away. Her pulse quickened beneath his fingers. "You and I have unfinished business to discuss."

She made no attempt to conceal her displeasure as she plopped back into her chair, forcing him to release her. She picked up her fork and stabbed it viciously into her dessert. No doubt she'd rather plant the tines in him.

Looking between him, Madeline and Ian, Amelia hesitated. Dominic suspected she'd stay with the slightest encouragement from her friend, but Madeline waved her away. "It's okay. I'll be right there."

Moments later the door closed behind Ian and Amelia. Dominic refilled Madeline's wineglass and then his own. "How long did your engagement last?"

"None of your business." She shoved a bite of confection between her lips and the urge to taste it on her tongue swelled within him. Normally he didn't care for sweets, but licking the rich cream from Madeline's skin appealed. Immeasurably.

"Shall I call back your friend? She seemed quite willing to provide information."

"And you were not in the least bit subtle in prying my personal data out of her."

He couldn't stop a smile. "I don't think she noticed."

"*I* noticed."

"How long?"

She huffed out a breath and pushed away her plate. "Six years."

"Six *years?*" What man could possibly allow such an eternity to pass without claiming Madeline as his own? He and Giselle had waited three years, but that was because Giselle had been too young when their engagement began. "Your fiancé had commitment issues?"

"Aren't you a smart guy to figure that out so quickly. It took me a lot longer."

"So you once believed in love? And now you don't."

"Nice analysis, Dr. Freud. Can I go now?"

"How did you make the transition?"

She blinked. "Huh?"

"How did you make yourself accept the idea of a life without a connection or bond with someone who actually gives a damn about you?"

Her lips parted and her eyes widened. "Holy moly. You're a romantic."

He debated telling her about the sterile selection process underway at home, but what point would that serve? It certainly wouldn't aid his cause in getting Madeline back into his bed and stockpiling his need for passion before he commenced a life without it. And since their relationship was temporary, what happened in Montagnarde would not affect her.

"I am tired of one-night stands. I wish to have someone share my bed for reasons other than duty, greed or fleeting attraction."

"Why bother? You'll just get disappointed in the end."

"My parents have been married for almost forty years and each of my sisters for nearly a decade. Their marriages are strong and happy."

"For now." She grabbed her wine and took a healthy sip. "My parents were married for thirty-five years before my father walked out."

The pain and sadness in her eyes tightened his chest. "Why did he leave?"

She rose. "Does it matter?"

"Apparently it matters to you. I've heard children often blame themselves for their parents' divorce."

"There you go again. Practicing psychology without a license. Don't they have laws against that in Monaco?"

But the sudden rigidity of her posture told him he'd hit a nerve. "Do you blame yourself?"

"Of course not," she replied too quickly. "I was only ten."

He captured her chin, lifted her face until she met his gaze, and repeated, "Do you blame yourself?"

She glared at him for a full thirty seconds before her lids lowered and her shoulders sagged on a sigh. "They were married twenty-five years before I came along. A menopause surprise baby. So yes, for most of my life I wondered if my arrival had upset the balance."

She shook off his hand, and hugging herself, moved to the window. "After my father died I finally found the courage to ask my mother what really happened. According to her they split because of indifference. They just fell out of love. Neither cared enough about the other to fight for their marriage, but they fought about anything and everything else. I was actually relieved when Daddy moved out and the shouting stopped."

She was tough, a fighter, and yet at the moment she seemed fragile and lost. Struggling with the urge to take her in his arms, for he doubted she would welcome his comforting embrace, Dominic joined her by the glass.

"Did you feel the same indifference for your lover?"

"What!" She pivoted to face him with her mouth agape.

"You did not love him enough to push forward with your wedding plans, and yet you did not dislike him enough to end your engagement. It appears he suffered the same indifference." He shrugged. "I would not wish for such a passionless relationship."

"It wasn't passionless," she said through clenched teeth.

"No? Did you not say last night that you had never had so many orgasms in one night nor found such pleasure? Tell me, Madeline, did you hunger for his touch the way you do for mine?"

A white line formed around her flattened lips and her face turned red. "My relationship with Mike is none of your business."

"I have heard most women choose men like their fathers."

The color drained from her cheeks and she actually staggered back a step. "What does that have to do with us? Because you sure as heck aren't looking for anything long-term with me."

He'd be damned if he knew why understanding Madeline Spencer was so important when she would be gone from his life in a matter of days. "No. As I have said before, I regret that here and now is all I can offer you."

And for some reason that left him feeling more dissatisfied and trapped by his life than he had in a very long time.

<u>Six</u>

Madeline stumbled midjog Tuesday morning when she saw her face on the cover of a tabloid paper.

She jerked to a halt on the cushioned running track along Boulevard du Larvotto and stared in dismay at the newsstand rack. Not one, but two papers carried photos of her and Dominic on their covers. She moved closer to examine the pictures of the two of them leaving the boat. With her hair tucked beneath her hat, her sunglasses covering part of her face and her profile angled away from the cameras, only her mother and closest friends would recognize her beside Dominic, who looked tall and commanding and royal.

Boy, had she misread him.

The captions were in French...or maybe Italian. She had no idea what they said. She reached into her shorts pocket for the euros she'd brought along to buy a bottle of water at the end of her run and picked up a copy of each paper. Her hands shook as she paid the man at the newsstand and accepted her change.

Hopefully Candace or Stacy would be able to translate. But were they awake yet? Despite their late nights here in Monaco, Madeline couldn't seem to break her wake-at-dawn habit.

With her plan to burn off the surplus of calories she'd consumed recently with a long morning run derailed, she rolled the papers into a baton and jogged back to the hotel. She let herself into the suite. Silence greeted her. None of her suitemates were awake. But she couldn't wait. She had to know what the articles said now.

So much for avoiding His Royal Hemorrhoid today by ducking out of the hotel early.

Returning to the hall she marched the length of the plushly carpeted corridor to Dominic's door and mashed the doorbell long and hard. He'd gotten her into this mess. It would serve him right if she woke him.

The door opened. "Good morning, Ian. Where is he?"

She tried to enter, but Ian's bulk blocked her way. "Prince Dominic is unavailable."

"Make him available."

The burly chest swelled. "Mademoiselle—"

"Let her in," Dominic's deep voice called from inside.

Five heartbeats later Ian stepped aside. Could he be a little more obvious that he didn't want her here? Madeline plowed past him only to jerk to a halt at the sight of a black-robe-clad Dominic sitting at the table with coffee and a newspaper. The silky fabric gaped as he rose, revealing a wedge of tanned chest dusted in golden curls. Below the loosely tied belt his legs and feet were bare.

Was he naked under there?

Get over it. You've already seen him naked and you see naked men at work every day.

With no small effort she pried her gaze upward. Burnished stubble covered the lower half of his face. His hair was mussed and his pale eyes curious. Her mouth dried and her pulse quickened. Clearly her body had not received the message from her brain that she was totally and completely over him and that there would be no more nookie.

"Good morning, Madeline. You are eager for my company today. That bodes well for our time together."

The devil it did. Her hands fisted. Paper crinkled, reminding her why she'd come. *The tabloids.* She crossed the room, thrust them at him and then after he took them, she retreated to the opposite end of the table.

His gaze traveled from her hastily braided hair to her chest in a snug tank top and breast-flattening jog bra and then down her bare legs to her running shoes. She'd dressed the way she always did for a workout, but suddenly she became uncomfortable with her skimpy attire and lack of makeup. Maybe she should have changed before coming here.

No. You are not trying to attract him anymore.

Tugging at the hem of her very short shorts, she cleared her throat. "What do they say?"

He unrolled the papers, scanned one and then the other, his lips compressing more with each passing second, and then his gaze returned to hers. "Our affair has become public knowledge. The good news is they haven't printed your name which means they don't know it yet. There is only speculation as to whom I'm seeing."

"But what do they say *exactly?*"

His frown deepened. He gestured to first one tabloid and

then the other. "The Prince's Paramour and The Prince's Playmate. Shall I translate the articles for you?"

"No." Her stomach churned. Why had she insisted on knowing what the tabloids said? Because she'd never bought into the ignorance is bliss theory—especially since Mike. But suddenly she wished she did. Gulping down rising panic she asked, "Why would anyone care about me? I'm a nobody."

"When you became a prince's lover you became a person of interest."

She felt as if she'd swallowed a gallon of seawater. A little queasy. A *lot* uncomfortable. "I did not sign on for that."

"Would you like coffee?" He gestured to the tray on the table. A second cup already had coffee in it. A third remained empty. She glanced at the frowning, dark-suited Ian. Was he more than an employee? And what about the missing Makos? Was the third cup for him?

Who cares? This is all about you, remember? Your mistake. Your humiliation. Your fraying credibility.

She turned back to Dominic. "I don't want coffee. I want to be left alone. By the paparazzi. And by you. I have things to do and places to see and a reputation to protect."

"Too late, I'm afraid. I will arrange for someone to guard you, but until he is in place you might wish to avoid crowded tourist attractions or risk being cornered by the paparazzi."

Guard her? Oh, please. "*Hello.* I am a tourist. I want to see the sights. I still haven't found a gift for my mother, so I *will* see them. And I don't want anyone shadowing me." She tugged at her braid. "What can we do?"

One shoulder lifted in a shrug. "Ride it out."

How could he be so laid-back? "I don't want to be branded as your mistress in the papers."

"I would have preferred to avoid it, as well, but what's done is done."

"Fix it, Dominic. Make them print a retraction or something."

"Demanding a retraction would only draw more interest. I am sorry, Madeline. We will do what we can to conceal your identity from the press so you will not be bothered once you return home, but I can offer no guarantees."

She groaned and a heavy weight settled on her chest. This could *not* follow her back to Charlotte. The whispers, abruptly stalled conversations and questions about her judgment had barely stopped from the Mike debacle.

"Your Highness, we could return to Montagnarde," Ian suggested.

Madeline's muscles tensed. Why? She wanted to be rid of Dominic. Didn't she?

She turned on Ian. "You called him Damon on the boat. Why get prissy now?"

When Ian remained silent Dominic explained, "That was before you knew my identity. Ian is a stickler for protocol in public."

"One, I have slept with you, so I'm not 'the public.'" She marked the words with quotation marks in the air. "Two, if he hadn't called the cops then we would not be having this conversation."

Dominic flung the papers on the table and closed the gap between them in three long strides, stopping so close she could smell his unique scent, feel the heat radiating from his body and see each individual blade of morning beard on his jaw and upper lip.

"Three," he continued, "if I had not misled you then four, you would not have threatened me, and Ian would not have called the police. We come full circle. Protecting me is his job."

We all share the blame, but the lion's share is mine because I am the one who began the masquerade."

Good point. And as much as she hated to admit it, Dominic's willingness to accept part of the blame surprised and impressed her. She was used to guys who shucked responsibility for their mistakes whenever possible. For example, the way Mike had blamed her for his cheating.

She pressed her fingertips to her temple. This was not turning out to be a good day. "What are our options?"

He caught her hand and carried her fingers to his lips. A shock wave of awareness swept over her before she snatched her hand away. "We could remain sequestered in my suite for the remainder of your stay in Monaco."

Temptation swamped her. It took a second to force her lungs to fill and oxygenate her brain enough for reason to return. "Not going to happen. I didn't come to Monaco to hide out in a hotel. And since I may never get back to Europe I plan to see some of it—which is why I wanted a tour guide."

"Then we will keep as low a profile as possible and continue as we had originally planned once additional staff is in place."

"Is that doable?"

"It is the way I live my life. Being watched or followed is unavoidable. In the future you might wish to consider that before venturing out alone, and I would suggest you not sunbathe topless unless you want the paparazzi to enjoy your beautiful breasts as much as I do."

His compliment was lost in a tidal wave of heart-sinking, skin-prickling panic. She hugged her arms across her chest. Had anyone been watching her this morning? What about yesterday when she'd sneaked out of the hotel at the crack of dawn and hidden out in a cybercafe until she could tour the

Monaco Porcelain Factory? Had someone been watching last night when she'd returned to the hotel and been immediately whisked up to Dominic's suite by Makos? The thought gave her the creeps.

"Join me for breakfast, Madeline."

The way he voiced the invitation, low and husky and intimate, caused her pulse to spike despite her concerns.

Good grief. Haven't you learned anything?

"I have to get back for Candace's morning meeting and to get the details of some ball thing from Stacy."

The doorbell chimed. His long fingers curled around her upper arm, infusing heat into her chilled muscles. "Come into my bedroom."

She tried and failed to yank free. "Have I been too subtle? I'm. Not. Interested."

"Breakfast has arrived. Would you prefer the server report that you were in my suite when I was not dressed?"

Ugh. "That kind of thing happens?"

"Yes. Hôtel Reynard is one of the best chains in the world for screening employees, but it is wise to be cautious."

"You mean paranoid." She shook off his hand and reluctantly accompanied him to the adjoining room. A king-size bed covered in tangled tan sheets dominated the space. The burgundy-and-gold paisley spread lay crumpled at the foot. They'd left the bed on the boat in a similar condition. Her body flushed hot and her clothing clung to her dampening skin.

Excuse me. You're over him. Remember?

He closed the door, leaned one shoulder against it and folded his arms over his chest. The move separated the fabric of his robe. "Tell me about the ball."

She forced her eyes away from the triangle of skin and the barely tied knot at his waist. "Not much to tell. I found a note from Stacy this morning saying there's going to be a ball Saturday night and that Franco is buying our gowns. That's all I know."

"Le Bal de L'Eté, a charity event which opens the season at the Monaco Sporting Club, is this weekend. Who is Franco?"

"Stacy's…friend." Her suitemate was having a passionate vacation fling, the kind Madeline had hoped to have, but—

"I don't like another man buying your dress."

"Tough." Through the door she heard the sounds of the room service cart being rolled into the dining area, the rattle of dishes and the low hum of voices, and then the cart leaving.

"I'll purchase your gown."

"And won't that look great in the tabloids? I'm no man's kept woman."

"And yet you would let this Franco pay for your dress."

She'd only met the sexy French chocolatier a couple of times, and normally she wouldn't let a stranger buy her clothing, but Franco only had eyes for Stacy. "He doesn't expect anything in return."

"You believe I would buy gifts for you to coerce you back into my bed?"

"We both know you want me there." And she was just as determined not to return. If he'd lied about one thing, he'd lie about another.

"Yes, I do. What's more, you want it, too."

Right.

Wrong! "That's quite a large ego you have there. Does Ian help you lug it around?"

Dominic's lips twitched and humor sparkled in his eyes. "I'll escort you to the ball."

"Oh yeah. That's being discreet. Forget it. I'm going with my suitemates. A girls' night out. And I plan to dance with every handsome man there." She cringed inwardly. That had sounded childish. But Dominic didn't own her and he'd better stop acting as if he did.

His nostrils flared and frustration thinned his lips. "You cannot evade me or the passion between us, Madeline."

"Watch me." Intent on a quick escape, she turned and reached for the doorknob.

In a flash his palm splayed on the door above her head, holding it shut. He leaned closer until the warmth of his chest against her back sandwiched her against the wooden panel. His breath stirred her hair seconds before his lips brushed her nape. Her lungs stalled and a shudder racked her. His morning beard rasped the juncture of her neck and shoulder, and then he traced a spine-tingling line down her backbone with one finger. Her senses rioted.

How can you still want him?

"You can't forget that night any more than I can," he whispered against her jaw.

The words scraped over her raw nerves and she swallowed hard. Almost every part of her being urged her to turn, wrap her arms around him, drag him to that rumpled bed and revel in the passion he offered. All she'd have to do is turn her head and their lips would touch.

The man's kisses could cause a nuclear meltdown.

But a lone brain cell reminded her of the hell she'd already lived through, of being made to look foolish and losing the respect of her coworkers and the uphill battle to regain it.

She squared her shoulders and tightened her fingers on the cool knob. "I might not have forgotten, but neither am I willing to become a topic of gossip again."

She yanked on the door. This time he let her go. "Be ready to leave for the shooting range as soon as your meeting ends."

She stopped halfway across the sitting room and pivoted to face him. "And if I'm not?"

"Have I ever mentioned Albert and I are well acquainted?"

Albert. Prince of Monaco. And he and Dominic were apparently on a first-name basis.

She was sunk.

"Hey, this isn't the way to the hotel," Madeline protested later Tuesday morning.

On the seat beside her in the hired car driven by Ian, Dominic angled to face her. His thigh touched hers. Touching meant sparks and sparks meant instant heat which she couldn't seem to control no matter how hard she tried. She inched away.

"You wished to purchase a gift for your mother."

Darn him for remembering that. "You could have asked if I wanted to go shopping."

He captured a dark curl, wound it around his index finger and tugged gently. She felt the pull deep inside. "You would have refused."

He had her there. But she'd just spent an hour matching him shot-for-shot at the shooting range and having more fun with their competition than she should have in the she'd-decided-to-hate-him circumstances. The man had a competitive streak that rivaled her own and a willpower-melting grin whenever he bested her. She needed a break from his magnetism.

"I also told you I'm having dinner with Candace at Maxim's tonight. So whatever you have planned had better be short and sweet."

"That's why we're taking a helicopter to Biot instead of driving."

A helicopter. She swallowed.

"I'm not crazy about helicopters." Not since a turbulent toss-her-cookies ride on a Life Flight chopper. Sure, she'd taken the helicopter taxi to Monaco from the Nice airport, but she'd been overexcited about being on foreign soil for the first time in her life and she'd had Dramamine in her system.

"I will be more than happy to distract you during the flight." His gaze dropped to her lips and her abdominal muscles contracted. She'd bet he would. She could guess how. But she wasn't kissing him again. Ever. Because his kisses sent her self-control AWOL.

"Would saying no make any difference?"

A smile teased his lips. "No. We'll land in time for lunch and then tour and shop. I'll have you back before dinner."

She sighed. It would serve him right if she barfed all over him. "Okay, you win."

"Always."

He really should try to rein in that cocky attitude. But darned if that smug smile didn't look good on him.

"What's so special about Biot?" she asked to distract herself as she reclaimed her hair. Each time he twined a curl around his finger she remembered the other things he liked to wrap it around and that wasn't good for her willpower.

"It's a small French village known for its pottery and hand-blown glass. Their earthenware production dates back to the Phoenicians, but since the 1960s Biot's bubble glass has gained international acclaim. My mother collects it. I thought yours might like it."

His mother. She didn't want to think about someone somewhere loving him. And she didn't want him to be thoughtful. He was a lot easier to dislike when he was arrogant, dictatorial and throwing his royal weight around. "You can force me to go with you, but you can't make me enjoy it."

"Have I mentioned how much I delight in your challenges?"

Five hours later Madeline stood in the shadows beneath a pointed archway of Biot's Place des Arcades and admitted she'd have to eat her words. Pleasantly tired and carrying a bag containing several carefully wrapped brightly colored pieces of bubble glass, she leaned against a sun-warmed stone wall and reluctantly looked up at Dominic.

He'd been an intelligent and amusing companion during this unwanted outing, and he'd taken her not to tourist traps, but to authentic out-of-the-way shops and a restaurant frequented by locals. His language and bargaining skills had been invaluable, and he wasn't exactly hard on the eyes. What more could a woman ask for in a date? If it hadn't been for his fib and his princeliness she could almost wish this idyllic period didn't have to end so soon.

"At the risk of inflating your already gargantuan ego, I have to confess, I enjoyed today. Lunch, the galleries, the museum…all of it."

"I'm glad." Dominic braced his shoulder on the wall beside her. He stood too close, but she couldn't seem to muster the energy to widen the gap between them.

He won points for not gloating.

They hadn't been bothered by paparazzi, and she'd only spotted Ian and Makos skulking in the background a few times. She hadn't even become ill on the helicopter flight because Dominic had applied acupressure to the inside of her wrist. A secret from the Montagnarde natives, he'd told her. Well, she'd studied acupressure, too, but she must have missed that chapter. Or maybe Dominic's touch had worked magic.

He slowly reached up and removed his sunglasses and then hers. Their gazes locked and held. The smile in his eyes faded and his pupils dilated with desire. Her pulse quickened and her mouth dried. After warning her to be on the lookout for paparazzi, surely he wouldn't—

His mouth covered hers. Tenderly. Briefly. Before she could react he swooped in again, cradling her jaw in his palm and settling in for a deeper taste. His tongue parted her lips and tangled with hers.

Need coiled tightly inside her, sending heat spiraling from her core to her limbs. She shouldn't be kissing him, shouldn't be savoring the hint of coffee on his tongue or the scent of his cologne. She shouldn't be curling her fingers into the rigid muscles of his waist or leaning into the warmth of his chest.

You definitely shouldn't be considering dragging him to the nearest inn.

Where was her remarkable willpower, her vow to keep their lips forever separate? Turning her head aside, she broke the kiss and gasped for air. She craved the man more than she did carbohydrates when PMSing. And that was saying something.

She gathered her tattered resistance and backed away. "We should go. I have to get ready for tonight."

And she had to brace herself for their next encounter, because she couldn't afford to let Dominic Rossi slip beneath her guard again.

Even if she could overlook his fib, a prince and a commoner had no future.

Not that she wanted one.

Seven

Time was running out.

Dominic snapped his cell phone closed Saturday night, shoved it in his tux pocket and inhaled deeply, but the constriction of his chest tightened instead of loosening.

"News?" Ian asked from beside him on the limo seat.

"The list of bridal candidates has been narrowed to three." Which meant Dominic's days of passion and freedom were numbered. He had to get Madeline back into his bed.

"This is not unexpected, Dominic."

That didn't mean he had to like it. "No."

"Perhaps your outings with Miss Spencer have spurred the council to make a decision."

"We have been discreet." As much as he hated sneaking in and out of back doors and service entrances, he'd willingly done so to spend time with Madeline. But this week she'd avoided all but the most casual of touches.

"The council won't give you the women's names?" Ian asked.

"No. They don't want me to interfere with the selection process." The council would make the decision, negotiate the diplomatic agreements, and then he would meet the woman and propose for formality's sake. The way it had been done for three centuries.

The car stopped in front of the Monaco Sporting Club. Ian climbed out first. Dominic remained seated. He didn't want to waste an evening rehashing the same shallow conversations or battling the predatory females whom he could not afford to offend. He would prefer to be alone in his suite—in his bed—with Madeline. But Madeline would be here, and her vow to dance with every male present chafed like an over-starched shirt. Absurd since once his bride-to-be was chosen he would have no claim on Madeline. He would tell her goodbye and immediately fly off to fulfill his duty to his country and his promise to his father to continue the tradition and the monarchy of Montagnarde.

The weight of his obligations had never weighed as heavily on his shoulders as it did now.

Ian's face appeared in the open door. "Your Highness?"

Dominic climbed from the car and entered the gala. The upper echelons of European society were out in full force at the charity ball. These were the very people he needed to court and attract to Montagnarde. At the moment he couldn't care less. He scanned the crowd, searching for Madeline, but didn't see her. An acquaintance greeted him. Dominic forced a smile and commenced his job as businessman and ambassador for his country.

But as he worked the room, politely fending off unwanted advances, some subtle, some not, he wondered if his future bride was among the women in attendance tonight, for this was very likely the pool from which she would be chosen. He found the prospect unappealing since none of the women attending the ball attracted him in the least.

Three-quarters of an hour later movement at the entrance drew his attention. Madeline and her suitemates had arrived. Urgency made his heart pump harder.

Madeline had pulled her dark hair up, leaving her shoulders bare. Her drop-dead sexy black dress molded itself to the curves of her exquisite figure. When she stepped forward a slit opened almost to the curls concealing her sex to reveal one sleek, tanned leg. She turned as a dark-haired man claimed the woman beside her, and Dominic stifled a groan. Other than straps encircling her shoulders in a figure eight, the back of her dress left the smooth line of her spine completely bare to just above the crease of her bottom.

Beautiful, seductive Madeline. He had to have her. Tonight.

"Prince Dominic," a high-pitched voice said nearby.

He blinked and looked back at the woman whose red talons gripped the sleeve of his tuxedo jacket. He couldn't recall her name. "Yes?"

"I asked if you'd like to see me home tonight." She followed the words with an inviting pout and a flutter of false eyelashes which did nothing for him.

"I am honored, mademoiselle, but I must decline. I have a previous engagement. Excuse me." He bowed and made his way toward Madeline only to be delayed again and again. His frustration grew. He had to reach Madeline before another man claimed her.

She was his.

For now. And he would have his fill of her before his desolate future consumed him.

* * *

How hard could it be to *not* kiss a guy? Madeline silently fumed as she stood near the entrance of the exclusive La Salle Des Étoiles.

She "not kissed" guys every day. Dozens of them. Coworkers, patients, paramedics, her letter carrier, for Pete's sake. So what was the big deal about not kissing one more? But that was her goal.

She'd succeeded Monday night, thanks to dinner with Dominic being interrupted by an urgent call from the palace which he'd had to take.

She'd blown it Tuesday in Biot, but she'd managed to keep her lips from straying on Wednesday when he'd surprised her with a behind-the-scenes tour of the Prince's Palace, including rooms not open to the general public. She'd stuck to her guns again on Thursday because Candace and Amelia—bless 'em—had run interference by accompanying her on the visit Dominic had arranged to Princess Grace Hospital. Afterward, her suitemates had dragged her out for a night at the theater sans Dominic.

But resisting him hadn't been easy. Each day his hungry gaze had gobbled her up bite by bite, leaving her more than a little ravenous and close to bingeing on the taste, scent and feel of him.

Thank God for Friday when she'd had the good fortune to avoid Dominic completely. She hadn't been hiding *exactly.* She'd kept herself busy away from the hotel by shopping and doing wedding minutiae with her suitemates from breakfast until bedtime.

She'd been so happy to evade temptation that she hadn't even minded the reminders of her own aborted engagement. In fact, she'd barely thought of Mike, the mistake. But that was because another man had planted his flag in her subconscious and claimed her thoughts. Damn Dominic Rossi for that.

Her gaze collided with Dominic's across the haute couture and jewel-encrusted crowd of Le Bal de L'Eté and her breath caught. Speak of the devil. Her luck had apparently run out.

With his regal bearing, aristocratic bone structure and wealth of confidence, no one looking at him now would ever doubt his royal lineage. The man commanded attention without even trying, and he turned wearing a tux into an art form.

A blonde so thin the wind could blow her away stood beside him with a rapt expression on her immobile Botox-filled face. He flashed a smile at her, said a few words then broke free and headed in Madeline's direction only to be side-lined by a squinty redhead and then a big-toothed brunette whose invitation to dance horizontally as well as vertically was obvious from clear across the room.

Madeline gritted her teeth and turned her back on the prince and his fawning females. She was not jealous. Nope. Not her. He could do the mattress merengue with every other woman in the room for all she cared.

"See anybody you recognize?" she asked wide-eyed Amelia. If there was a celebrity or royal in attendance, Amelia would be able to name him or her.

"Are you kidding? This place is a who's who smorgasbord. And I'm sorry to say, that includes Toby Haynes. I cannot believe Vincent sent that race car Casanova to babysit us."

"Vincent meant well, and Toby is his best man." Vincent had been working overseas, but moments ago he'd surprised Candace by arriving at the ball unexpectedly. He'd quickly swept his bride-to-be onto the dance floor where the two gazed at each other with so much love in their eyes it made Madeline uneasy. She'd once believed herself that much in love, and how she'd survived the aftermath was still a mystery. She could guarantee she'd never let herself care like that again.

"He should know we're old enough to stay out of trouble."

Amelia's comment made Madeline shift guiltily in her stiletto heels. The edges of her heavy black sequined dress abraded her skin. She hadn't managed to stay out of trouble, but she'd neglected to fill her suitemates in on the embarrassing details. Amelia knew nothing more than what Dominic had told her—that Madeline had threatened him. Her friend didn't know the threat involved an actual knife against his princely throat or firing a gun over his royal head.

Madeline followed Amelia's disgusted gaze toward the NASCAR driver who'd been a thorn in her friend's side since their first day in Monaco. Thanks to Candace's misguided matchmaking attempts, Madeline had dated Toby a couple of times back in Charlotte. She'd quickly labeled him a player and lost interest. The attraction—or lack thereof—was mutual.

Toby was a nice enough guy and definitely good-looking, but as far as she could tell he was serious about racing and little else. Amelia, on the other hand, had taken an intense dislike to Toby during Vincent's hospital stay last year when Toby had been a frequent visitor to the burn unit. No amount of prying—subtle or otherwise—on Madeline's part had uncovered the reason for the tension between those two.

"Do you see those women drooling over him?" Amelia grumbled. Amelia was the most easygoing woman Madeline had ever met, and seeing her friend bristle and hiss like an angry cat was totally out of character. There had to be a reason.

The back of Madeline's neck prickled, and it had nothing to do with Toby spotting them and extracting himself from the women clustered around him to head in their direction. "What is it with these chicks and their sycophantic admiration? Do they have no pride? And don't even get me started on how these guys are sucking up the adulation as if it's their due."

"Good evening, Amelia, Madeline." Dominic's baritone behind her confirmed the reason for her uneasiness. Her bones turned soupy. She cursed her wilting willpower. So much for her plan to avoid the man who had the power to kiss her right out of her clothes.

"Dominic, Amelia would like to dance," she said as she turned. She tried to keep her gaze on his blue eyes, but she couldn't help soaking up the breadth of his shoulders.

"Madeline!" Amelia protested.

"It's either Dominic or Toby. Take your pick." Madeline indicated the approaching driver with a tilt of her head.

Amelia's eyes widened with panic. She looked beseechingly at Dominic and even curtsied. "I would love to dance, Your Highness."

With a polite smile Dominic inclined his head and offered Amelia his arm. "Dominic, please. I would be delighted, Amelia."

But his eyes promised Madeline retribution as he led her friend away.

Ha! He couldn't get even if he couldn't catch her. She'd make a point of dancing in the arms of other men all night—even if she had to ask them herself. She'd chosen a dress which guaranteed their answers would always be yes.

Toby reached Madeline's side moments later. His appreciative gaze zipped from her upswept hair down her black form-fitting dress to her silver sandals before he met her gaze. "If your goal is to bring these European guys to their knees, I'll bet my new engine you'll succeed. You look good enough to make me reconsider making a run for you myself, Madeline."

A girl—this one anyway—liked to have her ego stroked even

if she suspected the compliment generated from habit rather than genuine interest. "Thanks, Toby. You look sharp, too."

Toby Haynes might be blond-haired and blue-eyed and of a similar height and athletic build to Dominic, but that's where the likeness ended. Even though both men wore what were probably custom-tailored tuxes, Toby had rough edges aplenty whereas Dominic was smooth, polished perfection. But Toby didn't trip her hormonal switches. Dominic, regrettably, did.

"Who's the stiff?"

She didn't pretend not to understand Toby's question. How could she, since his eyes practically shot fire toward the man in question? "Prince Dominic Rossi of Montagnarde."

"Montag—what? Never heard of the place. Must not have a race track."

Nice to know she wasn't the only geographically challenged one present. "Montagnarde. It's a country somewhere between Hawaii and New Zealand."

"Wanna dance?"

Not the smoothest invitation she'd ever had, but it beat standing near the entrance like a wallflower. "Sure. Why not?"

Toby led her onto the floor and swept her into the flow of other dancers with skill she wouldn't have expected from a car jockey. "You're pretty light on your feet."

He grimaced. "Comes with the territory. For the most part NASCAR drivers only drive two days a week. Qualifying and race day. The rest of the time we're on the road schmoozing for the sponsors. Reynard Hotels loves swanky parties like this."

And Vincent Reynard's hotel chain sponsored Toby's racing team. "You don't?"

"Depends on the reason I'm there." He drew alongside Amelia and Dominic. "Hey, buddy, switch?"

Madeline's insides snarled. She should have known a competitive guy like Toby would have an agenda. But it was too late to escape the man she'd hoped to avoid.

Dominic stopped and released Amelia. "Certainly. Thank you for the dance, Amelia."

He bowed slightly.

Darn, she liked that stupid little bow.

Toby whisked her none-too-happy friend away.

Madeline stood in the middle of the floor and met Dominic's gaze while the other guests drifted past them. "I don't want to dance with you."

"The floor is the best place for us unless you are ready to leave." Dominic's hand captured hers. The only way to escape his unbreakable grip was to cause a scene—not part of the plan if she wanted to avoid more publicity.

"Are you kidding me? I just got here."

He pulled her into the circle of his arms and spread his palm on her naked back just above her buttocks. Her pulse tripped. She hoped her feet wouldn't embarrass her by doing likewise.

She searched for a distraction from the heat of his hand on her skin and tried to ignore the slide of his thighs against hers as he guided her across the floor. "Where's the towering twosome? Did you check your bodyguards at the door?"

"Ian and Makos remained outside as did Fernand."

"Who is Fernand?"

"Your protection."

She stumbled then and fell into his broad chest. His arm banded around her waist, welding her to the hot, hard length of his torso and keeping her there. He continued dancing without missing an orchestral beat. "My what?"

"You have had security since Wednesday."

"You've had someone following me?" The erotic rasp of

his tuxedo jacket sleeve against her back tightened her throat, making her words come out in a husky whisper.

"I told you I would."

"Yes, but…" She rewound the reel of events in her head. Had she done anything she wouldn't want reported back to Dominic? Because she'd bet his spy guy was doing exactly that. "I haven't seen him."

"You weren't supposed to." His smooth-shaven chin brushed her temple as he executed a series of quick turns that required her to cling to him or fall on her face. Ballroom dancing had never been her thing, but she had to admit following his lead was easier than expected. Good thing, since sprawling on the floor given her attire, or lack thereof, would be humiliating.

"Why do I need a shadow?"

"There are those who might believe that because you're my lover—"

Stumble. "I'm not anymore."

"—you might be a valuable negotiating piece," he continued as if she hadn't interrupted.

Fear crept up her spine like a big, hairy spider. She leaned back to look into his eyes. Unfortunately, that pressed their hips together. "I'm in danger because I slept with you?"

"Probably not. As you pointed out, Montagnarde is off the radar for most, but I prefer to be proactive rather than reactive. And while you are mine I will protect you."

The possessive words made her skin tingle. And then she remembered to object. "I. Am. Not. Yours."

The hand on her back lifted, giving her a momentary reprieve and an opportunity to fill her wheezy lungs, but then Dominic traced the edge of her dress from her shoulder to the base of her spine. The tips of his fingers slid just beneath the fabric and his short nails raked lightly across the top of her cheeks. She shivered, cursed her traitorous hormones and sent out a mental SOS to her willpower. Wherever it might be.

"You look lovely tonight. Very sexy. Come back to my suite with me, Madeline," his deep voice rumbled in her ear.

Stumble. He caught her even closer—something she would not have believed physically possible five seconds ago. Even through the heavy chain mail weight of her dress she could feel his thickening arousal against her belly. Flames of desire flickered through her and her resistance softened like warm candle wax. She was so close to melting it wasn't even funny.

But the man had broken rule number one. He'd lied to her.

And still…she wanted him. Shamelessly.

Girl, you are absolutely pitiful.

But she couldn't help remembering how good it had been between them, how amazingly wonderful he'd made her feel or how he listened to every word as if she were going to utter the secret to world peace in her next sentence.

You are in serious trouble.

"Get me off this floor," she said through clenched teeth.

"Or else what?" A smile played on his lips as he pulled her into another series of complicated make-her-cling-to-him steps. "You'll pull a weapon? Because I don't see where you could possibly conceal one beneath that dress. It caresses your curves the way I want to."

Stumble. Help. She could not argue and concentrate on fancy footwork at the same time. She planted her feet, shoved his rock-hard chest and yanked free of his hold. "Do you really want to test me here and now, Dominic?"

Ignoring the curious stares of those around her, he held her gaze as if considering calling her bluff, but then inclined his head and led her toward the edge of the floor. They had barely stepped out of the crowd when a woman wearing a take-me-I'm-yours smile appeared in front of him.

"*Bonsoir,* Your Highness. Remember me?"

Dominic made introductions, but Madeline only half listened to the simpering blonde's chatter about past parties and people Madeline knew nothing about. She scanned the well-heeled guests looking for her suitemates and a possible rescue. She spotted Stacy and Franco and Vincent and Candace, but both couples were totally wrapped up in each other. There was no sign of Amelia and/or Toby.

"...come by my apartment later?" the blonde said.

Huh? Madeline blinked in disbelief and tuned back into the conversation. Had that she-cat just propositioned Dominic despite his hand planted firmly on Madeline's waist?

Hello! What am I? Invisible?

"Excuse us, Dominic was about to get me a glass of champagne." She grabbed his arm and urged him toward the bar and then jerked to a stop. *Argh. Is your brain on hiatus?* She'd wanted to escape him, and she'd just wasted a perfect opportunity. She should have let the she-cat have him.

So why didn't you?

She had a feeling she wouldn't like the answer.

"Thank you," he said.

Before she could tell him to take his gratitude and shove it, the catty incident replayed itself again and again and again. Different woman. Same pounce. Every three yards. Jeez, fighting off the felines was exhausting. Forget champagne. At the rate they were going she'd need an entire bottle of gin to wash down the fur balls by the time they reached the bar.

Patience deserted her and she yearned to scratch a few

overly made-up eyes out. While Dominic clearly did not enjoy or encourage the attention, he remained unfailingly polite each time. Most men would have been ecstatic to hear so many come-ons in a single evening, but not him. Why was that? Was his little black book already full? Or did he consider Madeline a sure thing?

She found the encounters pretty darn insulting since it meant these pedigreed felines didn't consider her competition, and she'd had enough.

"Excuse me. I guess you missed the fact that he's with me," she interrupted a woman about to spill from her rhinestone-studded collar—um, dress.

"Dominic, *dahling*," Madeline purred in a throaty voice similar to the ones his accosters had used, "I could use that double martini you promised me right about now."

Laughter lurked in his eyes as they said their goodbyes, and then Madeline nudged him not toward the bar but toward a quiet corner. "Is there some kind of contest to see who carries home the richest prize at the end of the evening?"

The first genuine smile she'd seen in an hour curved his lips. "You have discovered the secret."

"Is that why you wanted to stay on the dance floor? To avoid the stalking women?"

"An apt description."

"Why don't you just tell them to get lost?"

He glanced toward the gathering and then back at her. "I can't."

"Some princely code or something?" But she didn't wait for his answer. "If it's always like this, then why do you come to these things?"

"Usually I come because I want to entice their business to Montagnarde." His blue gaze held hers as he lifted her hand to his lips. "Tonight I came because I wanted to hold you in my arms."

Her knees weakened and the bottom dropped out of her stomach. The room seemed to fade until all that remained was him and the desire burning in his eyes. For her. In this room full of beautiful, elegant, worldly, predatory women, he wanted her.

"Good answer," she wheezed.

And why are you resisting?

She mentally smacked a palm against her forehead. She'd wanted a man to help her heal her fractured ego and rebuild her confidence. Dominic did that. He made her feel feminine and desirable. He gave her multiple-o's.

He'd reminded her more times than she could count that here and now was all they'd have. But that was okay. More than okay. A brief vacation fling was exactly what she wanted.

It wasn't as if she'd let herself fall in love or imagine marrying him. Just as well since Dominic, like Prince Charles, probably had to marry a virgin. And she wasn't one. Not even close.

Between tonight, the incident with the paparazzi and having to sneak in and out back doors all week she could even understand Dominic's motivation for concealing his identity. But he was selling himself short if he truly believed these women wanted him only for his title and fortune. Dominic Rossi, Prince of Montagnarde, was a gorgeous piece of work, and every time she looked at him she recalled the perfection of his naked body and the way he made her body sing.

She'd bet the drooling females wanted a chance to do the same. Knowing she knew something the other more sophisticated women didn't made her feel just a teensy bit superior.

*And you're wasting time here when you could be getting
your hands on all that perfection.*

Her pulse quickened and her mouth dried. She tightened her
fingers around his. "Get me out of here, Prince, and you can
hold me in your arms without a ten-pound dress between us."

The flash of heat in his eyes nearly consumed her on the
spot. "As you wish."

Eight

Apparently the wealthy didn't wait for cabs or even valet service.

Within seconds of her shameless declaration Dominic had hustled her out of the gala and into a waiting limo which he'd summoned with one touch on his cell phone. She chose the bench seat facing the limo's rear window.

Dominic joined her instead of sitting across from her. From shoulder to knee the hot length of his body pressed her side as hot and hard as an iron. The door closed, sealing them in darkness and near silence, and then the car pulled away from the club.

She risked a glance at him and found his jaw muscles knotted and his gaze burning into hers. Hunger stiffened every line of his body, inspiring a similar tension in hers.

She'd never wanted anyone this badly. Digging her fingers into her tiny beaded purse and hoping to slow her racing pulse, she focused on the passing lights of Monte Carlo outside the window as the driver carried them toward the hotel. No luck.

She squirmed impatiently, but the only thing her wiggling accomplished was to make the slit in her dress part, revealing her leg from ankle to hip. Before she could adjust the gaping skirt she heard Dominic's sharply indrawn breath, and then his hand covered her knee. Ever so slowly his warm palm glided upward, his fingertips slipping beneath the edge of the heavy, sequined fabric. Her insides clenched. She'd very likely leave a puddle of desire on the seat if she didn't stop him.

She slapped a hand over his and leaned toward him to whisper in his ear. "What are you doing? Ian and the driver are right behind us."

"The privacy screen is closed and the speaker turned off. They can see and hear nothing." His fingers inched higher and his masculine scent filled her lungs with each shaky breath. "You wish me to stop?"

"Yes. No. Yes. I...don't know." She struggled to bring order to her scrambled thoughts. "Do you, um...do this often?"

A short nail scraped back and forth along the top of her thigh, each pass drawing closer to the spot aching for his touch. "I have never made love in a limo."

"Me, neither." But she was tempted. Seriously tempted. She forced her heavy lids to remain open. "We're almost at the hotel."

"Then I'd better hurry." His hand rose another inch and he found her wetness with the tip of his finger. Their groans mingled. "You're not wearing panties."

"Dress. Too. Tight," she whispered brokenly as he circled her center bringing her closer and closer to the brink. How did he do that so quickly? Arousal made it difficult to think and tension made her tremble. She covered his hand with hers, intent on stopping his audacious behavior…in a minute. "Dominic—"

"Shh. Come for me, Madeline," he whispered hoarsely.

"H-here?" Their hotel was less than a block away and privacy screen or not, Ian and the driver were only inches away.

"Now. I want you so wet that I can be inside you the moment we reach the suite."

His throaty words and talented fingers sent her flying. Her back bowed and her tush lifted off the seat as wave after wave washed over her. She bit hard on her bottom lip and fought to remain silent as her pleasure went on and on and on. When it finally ended she leaned heavily against his side.

His breathing sounded as harsh as hers in the insulated passenger compartment and she hadn't even touched him. To anyone who happened to glance in the rearview mirror or through the tinted windows, they probably looked like any other couple riding home from a ritzy party. No one would guess she'd just crash-landed from a trip to the stars.

"Your turn." She spread her palm on his thigh, but he stopped her wandering hand by lacing his fingers through hers and carrying her hand to his lips.

"Hold that thought." The limo stopped outside Hôtel Reynard's back entrance. Her body seemed heavy, melded to the upholstery. Dominic released her hand and straightened the folds of her dress. He squeezed her thigh and then released her. "Ready?"

"Are you kidding me? I don't think I can walk."

His low chuckle aroused her all over again. His breath teased her bare shoulder a second before his teeth lightly grazed her skin. In her hypersensitive state the brief contact sent a bolt of lightning straight to her womb. "If I carry you inside we'll definitely draw unwanted attention. Shall I ask the driver to circle the block?"

She sucked air into her deprived lungs and grappled for sanity. "No. I can't wait that long to have you inside me."

Dominic's breath whistled through clenched teeth. "Nor I."

Dominic had had sex before. Hot, sweaty, animalistic sex.

He'd even had sex with Madeline. But he'd never been as close to saying to hell with propriety and taking a woman regardless of their location. The limo. The elevator. The carpeted hallway outside his suite. He shook with need, and he couldn't remember the last time that had happened. Only Ian's scowling presence prevented him from taking action. Here. Now.

Madeline stood beside him in the hotel hallway without touching him. But her scent filled his lungs with every breath. Flowers. Lemon. *Sex.* He waited impatiently for Makos to do a security sweep of the suite. The moment the man gave the all's clear signal Dominic grabbed Madeline's hand and dragged her over the threshold, through the sitting room and into his bedroom. He shut the door in his bodyguards' faces, backed Madeline against the panel and slammed his mouth over hers.

She opened for him instantly, suckling his tongue and curling her fingers into his shoulders. She shoved at his tuxedo jacket and then tore at his tie and the buttons of his shirt without breaking the kiss. The garments landed on the floor behind him. With their lips still fused he raked his hands over the cool sequins of her dress searching feverishly but fruitlessly for the zipper. He gave up and tried to lift her skirt, but the fitted fabric clung stubbornly to her hips. He considered ripping it—this dress another man had bought—from her.

He wanted skin. Her skin. Against his. Now.

Madeline's nails scraped over him, drawing a line from his

Adam's apple to his navel, and then she palmed his erection through the fabric of his pants. Arousal detonated inside him. He released her mouth long enough to gasp, swear and demand, "Zipper."

"Here." She carried his hand across her breasts to her underarm. His fingers fumbled, found the tab, and tugged it to her hip. At a loss as to how to remove the seductive dress, he stepped back.

"Over my head."

He fisted the fabric, uncaring if he damaged it. He'd buy her another. A dozen. The weight of the garment surprised him. The moment the hem cleared her head he twisted and tossed it on a nearby chair. And then he turned back to Madeline and his heart slammed into his ribs like an airplane hitting a mountainside. He staggered back a step, two. His jaw went slack.

Naked, save a pair of silver high heels sharp enough to be classified as lethal weapons, she lifted her arms to pull pins from her hair. His lungs seized. He'd never seen a more seductive sight than Madeline, with her back arched and her breasts offered like a banquet. She stood with her long, lean legs slightly parted. Moisture glistened in the dark curls between her legs—moisture he'd created.

And he was about to lose it like a teenage boy.

He snapped his jaw closed and swallowed once, twice. But it did nothing to ease the constriction in his throat or the tightness in his chest. Need, painful in its intensity, clawed through him. One by one, long, dark ringlets fell over her shoulders as she released her hair, concealing her tightened nipples from his view. A criminal offense.

He captured a silky coil and painted a pattern over her puckered flesh and then brushed her hair aside to cup and caress her warm, satiny skin. Her breasts filled his hands, the nipples prodding his palms. He rolled the tips between his fingers until she whimpered and leaned against the door.

"Please, Dominic, don't make me wait." She reached for the waistband of his trousers.

He kissed her again, relishing the sharp bite of desire and the hunger fisting in his gut beneath her tormenting fingers. The moment she shoved his pants over his hips and curled her fingers around him he lifted her leg to his waist with one hand, cupped her bottom with the other and drove into her welcoming wetness. Her body clenched around him and her cries of pleasure filled his ears. He thrust again and again and again. More. Deeper. Harder. Faster. The heel of her shoe stabbed his buttocks. That little jab had to be the most erotic thing he'd ever felt.

Pressure built. He fought to hold on until her nails bit into his shoulders and she tore her mouth away from his to gasp his name. She shuddered in his arms and her internal muscles contracted. He could no more stop his own release than he could dam a volcano. His passion erupted, pulsing through him in mind-melting bursts. He muffled his groans against her warm, fragrant throat, and then sapped and sated, he fell against her.

When he recovered an ounce of strength, he braced his forearms on the door beside her head and lifted his sweat-dampened body scant inches from her torso. The arms she'd looped around his neck kept him close—not that he intended going anywhere. He stared into her beautiful face. A smile curved her moist, swollen lips, and her lashes cast dark crescents on her flushed cheeks. He absorbed the image, imprinting it on his brain to drag out during the long barren years ahead.

Two more weeks won't be enough.

It must be.

Madeline deserved more than to be a prince's paramour. She deserved a man who would look past her prickly exterior to the soft heart she fought so hard to protect. She'd once believed in love, and the right man would make her believe again. But that man wasn't him, for no matter how empty his marriage might be he would abide by his vows and his duty to his country.

Chilling arrows of regret pierced him. Madeline deserved to be happy. Even if he couldn't be.

"Wow." Her lids fluttered open and her satisfied gaze met his. And then noting his expression, she stiffened and pleasure drained from her face. She pushed against his chest and uncoiled her leg from his hip. "What's wrong?"

He slipped from her body and then it hit him. "We didn't use protection."

His pulse kicked erratically. With hope? Of course not. His fate was sealed and he'd accepted it.

But what if he, like Albert of Monaco, fathered a child out of wedlock? Would paternity and a potential heir excuse him from an arranged marriage? No. Tradition and the council demanded a bride of royal lineage. A pedigreed princess.

But a child would tie him to Madeline and give him an excuse to see her in the future even if he could not continue the affair.

She averted her face and wrapped her arms around her waist. "I'm on the Pill. So we're in the clear unless you lied about your health."

Why didn't that revelation fill him with relief? And why did the reminder of his dishonesty still sting? He'd had good reason for his deception, hadn't he?

No. If he'd learned anything from this it was that there was never a good reason for deceit. He would have to tell Madeline about his impending marriage. She deserved to know why he must let her go—this woman who'd brightened his days. But not now. When he said goodbye would be soon enough.

"I'm clean." He'd been poked and prodded, examined from top to bottom, inside and out, by the royal physicians. His health records would be provided for perusal to the family of the woman the council chose as his bride.

They could examine his vital statistics as they would a prize stallion. And like a stud for hire, he'd have no say over his mate. His obligation to provide heirs to the throne was a burden. Or was it a curse?

Madeline Spencer, jet-setter. Who would have believed it?

Madeline stared at the man standing beside her in the noonday sun in the tiny seaside town of Ventimiglia, Italy. She tried not to drool as sexy Italian words rolled off his tongue. Her tour guide extraordinaire and lover *magnifique*. Dominic.

He switched languages as easily as blinking whereas she'd struggled to pick up the necessary French phrases he'd taught her. He was probably discussing something as mundane as the weather with the merchant, but whatever he said made her want to jump him despite having left his bed just hours earlier.

She hated creeping from his suite every morning at sunup to sneak back to her room, but that was a small price to pay to keep their affair private and her name out of the tabloids. Thus far it had worked. Beyond those first couple of pictures there hadn't been more.

Curling her fingers against the urge to trace the veins on the thickly muscled arm closest to her, she focused her attention on the gold jewelry for sale. She'd already bought necklaces for her mother and Amelia and earrings for Candace and

Stacy from another vendor. Dominic, bless him, had handled the haggling and she'd ended up paying far less than she would have in the States.

An intricately engraved wide cuff bracelet caught her eye. She picked it up, saw the price and quickly put it down.

"You like it?" he asked.

"It's beautiful, but even if you talked him down to a fraction of what he's asking it would still be too expensive."

"I'll buy it for you."

She caught his hand as he reached for his wallet and stared at her floppy-hat-wearing reflection in his dark lenses. "It's bad enough that you won't let me split expenses for our outings. I'm not letting you spend more."

His jaw set in the stubborn line she'd come to recognize whenever she tried to insist on paying her way. She hadn't won a single one of those arguments, and she knew better than to expect to win this one, so she changed the subject. "What were you and the vendor discussing?"

His lips compressed, letting her know he hadn't missed her attempt at distraction. He said a few more words to the merchant and then placed his palm against Madeline's spine and guided her away from the table. He glanced over his shoulder—checking to see if Ian and Fernand followed, she suspected. It would be easy to lose them in the market-day crowd—even with her brightly colored hat, which had been chosen specifically to make her easy to track.

"I asked about market conditions. What improvements could be made and which features were absolute requirements. Montagnarde has many craftsmen. A marketplace like this would be a desirable asset to my tourism plans."

"But first you have to get the rich to visit Montagnarde and hemorrhage money." Normal people plotted to buy or pay off their homes. Princes, apparently, dreamed on a bigger scale. One night as they'd lain in the dark after making love, Dominic had told her about his development plan and his determination to move forward despite the elder council's refusal to support him.

"What did your American movie say? 'If you build it they will come?' It's the trickle-down theory. Each tourist generates income for the working class by creating multiple service jobs. Attract the big spenders and everyone will benefit. My investors and I are already constructing luxury hotels on two of the three islands. I would be interested in speaking with Derek Reynard about his family's chain constructing a third."

"I can probably arrange a meeting with Mr. Reynard, but Vincent, his son, is the director of new business development. And since I'm one of Vincent's wedding party, I know I can hook you up with him."

"I accept your offer and promise to reward you handsomely." His wicked grin sent a heat wave tumbling through her.

Dominic would make a great king one day. It made no sense for her to be proud of him and his forward-thinking agenda to bring tourists and jobs to his country. What he did once he left Monaco *and her* behind was none of her business. But there was no denying the pride swelling in her chest.

A gentle sea breeze caressed her skin as they walked hand in hand along the narrow street. She scanned the postcard view of red-roofed homes clinging to the hillside like pastel-colored building blocks. Ventimiglia was a combination of ancient history and New World charm, and she would have missed it without Dominic.

She'd never been happier than she had in the week since the ball. She'd spent the greater part of each day with Dominic. He'd taught her to windsurf and shown her bits of France: the carnival atmosphere of the summer jazz festival in Juan Les Pins; Grasse, the perfume capital of the world; and the blooming lavender fields and craft galleries in Moustiers Ste. Marie. Today when she'd only had a few hours to spare between bridesmaid's duties he'd surprised her with this jaunt to the Friday open-air market only twenty minutes from Monaco.

He thought nothing of day trips via helicopter or private jet, claiming the impromptu excursions to out-of-the-way places kept the paparazzi off their tails. She didn't want to tell him that she no longer needed to escape the wedding hoopla. Funny how the preparations didn't hurt anymore.

The only bacteria growing in the petri dish of Madeline's life was not knowing when Dominic would have to return to Montagnarde and when her time with him would end. He'd promised to show her Venice and Paris in the coming week—if he was still here. And that "if" kept her on a knife edge. Apparently, there was something pending in his country which required a nightly call from home—a call that left him increasingly tight-lipped and broodingly silent.

Madeline had learned a few techniques guaranteed to erase the frown from his face like the one currently deepening the worry lines on his forehead. She smiled and considered dragging him into an alley to distract him with one of those methods now, but a quick glance behind her revealed their bodyguards shadowing them.

Dominic lowered his sunglasses. His gaze found hers and the passion gleaming in his bedroom blue eyes made her steps falter. His fingers tightened around hers. "Do we need to take a siesta?"

Her heart skipped a beat. He read her so easily.

I could get used to this.

No, you can't. This is temporary and don't you forget it.

But there'd been a few times this week when a hint of yearning for more time with Dominic had slipped through her defenses. On each occasion she reminded herself that she no longer wanted forever with anyone. No more laying her heart on the line for some guy to trample. She'd abandoned dreams of children and a home in the suburbs the day Mike walked out.

Besides, Dominic was a prince, and even if she wanted more with him she couldn't have it.

"No can do. I have to get back for that thing with Candace's future in-laws."

His fingers stroked the inside of her wrist and her pulse quickened. "Too bad."

She didn't want to go to the dinner or the engagement party that followed and couldn't care less that the festivities would take place on the largest privately owned yacht in the world, which just happened to be docked in Monaco's harbor. Her reluctance had nothing to do with avoiding the reminders of her own aborted wedding and everything to do with not wanting to waste one moment of her remaining time with Dominic. "I could probably finagle an invitation for you."

He shook his head, adjusted the bill of his baseball cap and steered her away from a group of tourists studying him a little too intently. "The bride and groom should be the center of attention. You've seen what happens when I make an appearance."

She had and the surplus of kiss-up attitude nauseated her. But still, she didn't want to go without him.

Alarm skittered through her. Was she getting in too deep?

No. Dominic made her head spin in bed and out, but her growing attachment to him over the past three weeks could be blamed on the surreal circumstances of living the lifestyle of the rich and famous. Here she was a fish out of water. She clung to him because he made her feel as if she fit in and he smoothed her language difficulties. Once she was back in Charlotte and on familiar ground she wouldn't need him as a crutch or interpreter.

But she'd miss him.

Her heart beat faster and a peculiar emptiness spread through her like chilling fog. She was greedy for his company and she resented the interruptions. That's all it was.

She nibbled her lip as they approached the lot where they'd left the car. Maybe she should start weaning herself from him.

He leaned closer to murmur in her ear. "Come to my room after the party. Call my cell. No matter how late. I'll let you in."

Her mouth dried. "I was supposed to spend the night on the boat. Promise to make leaving worth my while?"

The glasses came off and his hungry gaze locked on hers. "I will make you beg for mercy."

And he could do it. Her breaths shortened and her skin dampened. The area between her legs tingled. "Deal."

Best-case scenario she had one more week with Dominic and wise or not, she intended to enjoy every second of it. Next Friday Candace and Vincent would have their civil ceremony followed by the church service on Saturday. Her friend would marry Vincent in the same church where Prince Rainier had shocked the world by marrying his commoner bride, Grace Kelly.

So royalty marrying a nobody could happen. It just wasn't going to happen to Madeline. And she was okay with that. Really.

She glanced at the man beside her and hoped she wasn't fooling herself, because on Sunday—only eight short days away—Madeline, Amelia and Stacy would fly back to the States. Madeline's days of living like a princess would be over, and soon all she'd have left were her memories of *Once upon a time in Monaco.*

Nine
<u></u>

"I thought you were known for speed," Madeline complained to Toby as she tried in vain to hurry him away from the yacht.

He'd graciously offered to walk her back to the hotel. No doubt when he'd made the suggestion he'd believed Amelia would be leaving with her. There was definitely something going on with those two, but her friend wasn't talking.

"I knew there was a reason we never slept together. You insult a guy's car before he even pulls it out of the garage," he replied in a teasing tone. He gripped her elbow and slowed her to his own leisurely pace. "Sweetheart, I always take it slow when it counts."

She snorted and rolled her eyes. "Oh please. Save the car jockey chatter for someone dumb enough to fall for it. You're lagging behind now, Haynes. Get the lead out."

He ignored her. She could have covered the next twenty yards of the jetty faster on her hands and knees. He must have sensed her impatience. "You have a hot date at midnight?"

Thinking of the night ahead, of hot embraces and even hotter kisses, Madeline's body heated. "I don't kiss and tell."

"Do your friends?"

The edge in his voice stopped her. "Should they? Because I swear, Toby, if you hurt Amelia—"

A darkly dressed figure separated itself from the shadows at the end of the jetty. Madeline's fight-or-flight response kicked in. She turned, ready to defend herself, but before she could act Toby hooked an arm around her waist and shoved her behind him so fast she almost fell off her four-inch heels. Her heart skipped for an altogether different reason when she recognized their "assailant."

Tension drained from her muscles. "Dominic. What are you doing here?"

"Waiting for you." Dominic's hair was slightly mussed and beard stubble shadowed his jaw. His gaze took in Toby's protective stance and his eyes narrowed.

Was that a possessive glint in his eyes? Darn the darkness. She couldn't tell. And it didn't matter anyway. Never in her life had she been more conscious of the countdown on her days with Dominic.

She stepped around Toby. "I don't think you two were introduced the night of the ball. Dominic, this is Toby Haynes, an American NASCAR car driver and team owner. Toby, Dominic Rossi, Prince of Montagnarde."

After a moment's hesitation, Dominic offered his hand. Madeline glanced from Dominic to Toby and back as the men shook hands. Had the testosterone tide swept in? And then with a sharp nod each man released simultaneously. Had she missed something?

Madeline touched Toby's forearm and Dominic stiffened beside her. For Pete's sake, he couldn't be jealous? Could he?

She knew Dominic cared about her. No man could be as passionate and unselfish a lover without some feelings for his partner, but love? Of course not. They both knew this was a dead-end relationship.

So why did a thrill race through her? She blinked away her irrational thoughts and blamed them on that last glass of champagne—the one she'd had to try because someone told her a single bottle of Krug Clos du Mesnil cost more than her monthly mortgage payment.

"Toby, I'm going to take a rain check on your offer of an escort back to the hotel."

"You're sure?"

"Absolutely. Good night and thanks. See you tomorrow."

After a moment's hesitation, Toby pivoted and headed back toward the yacht.

"Why will you see him tomorrow?"

"A wedding thing. Why are you really here, Dominic?"

"I was impatient for your company."

"Good answer."

His gaze caressed the deep décolletage of her halter-neck gown. "You look lovely. Very sexy. Very beddable."

Her nipples tightened in response to the desire in his eyes and his voice. "Thank you."

She glanced around. "I don't see Ian. Usually, I can spot him."

Was that a guilty flush on his cheekbones? "He's not here."

Surprise and concern rippled over her. "Voluntarily? Because the guy hates to let you out of his sight. I swear he'd be in the bedroom with us if given a choice. He still doesn't trust me."

Dominic's teeth flashed white in the moonlight, but his tight smile didn't completely erase the strain deepening the lines on his face. "He feels he failed me where you're concerned and it disturbs him."

He took her hand in his and guided her away from the harbor. "I used to be very good at giving Ian the slip. I decided to see if I still could."

"Hmm. So you have a few drops of rebel in your blue blood. I like that. And Fernand?"

"I informed him you'd been invited to spend the night on the yacht."

"I was. But I declined. As you well know." Amelia, Candace and Stacy had accepted. She glanced up and down the uncrowded area. Parts of Monaco rocked late into the night. This wasn't one of them. "Is it safe—for you, I mean—to wander the streets alone?"

Dominic shrugged. "Monaco is the safest country in the world. And I'm wearing tracking devices and carrying a panic button."

"So what's the plan? I'm guessing you didn't sneak out just to sneak back in again."

"Have I mentioned that I find your intelligence a turn-on?"

Her pulse spiked. "At least a dozen times. So what gives?"

"I'd like to walk through Monaco-Ville and enjoy the musicians and magicians of the Midsummer Night's Festival." He studied her shoes. "Or should we find a piano bar and sit?"

"Lucky for you, my shoes are not the kamikaze kind despite the stiletto heels." What had he told her? He wanted to feel like a man instead of a monarch? There weren't many gifts she could give a prince, but she could handle that request. She looped her arm through his. "Let's walk—if you're sure it's safe."

His hand covered hers on his forearm. He held her gaze. "I would never do anything to endanger you, Madeline."

"I know. You're a prince of a guy," she replied tongue in cheek. "Besides, you know you'll get lucky if you get me back to the hotel safely."

Dominic choked a laugh, dragged her into a shadowy alcove and covered her mouth with his. She *mmmphed* a protest through smiling lips, but dug her fingers into his waist and pulled him closer. Her smile faded as the heat of his body seeped into hers and hunger for Dominic took control of her brain. His lips were firm and his kisses hard and desperate with a dangerous edge that stopped just shy of being too rough.

The unusual aggression turned her on like nobody's business. By the time he lifted his head her heart raced and her legs quivered like a marathon runner's after crossing the finish line.

He leaned his forehead against hers and sucked in deep breaths. "Your puns are terrible. Stick to medicine."

"Your wish is my command, Your Royal Buffness," she replied with a wink and curtsied as she often had during the past five days. She only did it because she'd discovered how much kowtowing irritated him. As usual her smart-aleck quip made him chuckle. Good. She wanted to ease whatever somber mood had taken hold of him.

They strolled through the streets of Monaco-Ville for over an hour enjoying music, magic and sharing vendor foods like any other couple. But that was the catch. They weren't like any other couple and never could be. Tonight was a stolen moment—one they'd never repeat. The realization saddened Madeline enough to make her eyes burn and her chest hurt.

Dominic must have misinterpreted her silence as tiredness, for he waved down a taxi to carry them back to the hotel. When they arrived he silently escorted her inside, and then backed her against the wainscoted elevator wall, cradled her face in his hands and looked deep into her eyes.

"I will never forget our time together." The gravity of his voice made the fine hairs on her body rise.

"Neither will I."

And then he kissed her. She knew she was in trouble because she couldn't hold him tight enough, couldn't burrow close enough. And she didn't want to let him go.

Oh, my God. I'm falling for him.

Her stomach plunged as if the elevator had dropped to the basement. She gasped and broke the kiss.

The doors opened on the penthouse floor. Dominic threaded his fingers through hers and stepped toward the doors, but Madeline's muscles refused to engage. Had she been fooling herself by believing she could have an affair without her heart getting involved?

No. No. It's not love. It's only a crush. A crush due to circumstances, romantic settings, a man larger than life and a surplus of sexual satisfaction.

"Madeline?"

She blinked and swallowed. She wasn't dumb enough to fall for a prince. Was she?

Nope. Not love. Her rapid pulse, quickening breaths and the tension swirling in her belly were by-products of sexual arousal. Nothing more. And her chest ached only because Dominic had become a friend—a friend she'd soon have to say goodbye to.

Mentally kick-starting her muscles into motion, she traveled down the corridor beside him, tiptoed into the suite and then his bedroom. The covers looked rumpled, as if Dominic had been in bed but unable to sleep before coming after her. The bedside lamp cast a dim glow over the room. The digital clock read 2:00 a.m. She'd been up since 5:00 a.m. and should be exhausted, but energy hummed through her veins.

Behind her, the door lock clicked. She turned her head.

Dominic leaned against the panel with his hands behind his back. "Undress for me."

"Is that a royal command?"

"Need it be?"

"You first."

His lips twitched. He shook his head, but kicked off his shoes and reached for his belt. "Some man needs to tame you."

"*Pfft*. That'll never happen."

"I know. It's part of your charm." The belt slid free. He tossed it aside. "Your turn."

The longer this took the more time she'd have with him. Tomorrow—today—was Saturday. Candace didn't have a meeting and Madeline didn't have to be anywhere until noon. She and Dominic could sleep the morning away if they wanted. She kicked off her shoes and removed the silver clip from her hair.

Dominic removed his watch. She mirrored the action.

Without a word Dominic fisted his shirt, yanked the tails free and then reached beneath the fabric to unfasten his pants. His trousers slid to the floor. He kicked them aside.

All she could see was his great legs beneath the shirttail hem. "Tease. Two can play that game."

She reached beneath her dress and removed her panties. She shot them toward him like a rubber band. He caught the scrap of black lace, crushed it in his hand and stroked it across his cheek. He dropped her panties and shoved his briefs to the floor. A kick piled them on top of his discarded pants.

She released the button fastening the halter top of her dress at her nape and squared her shoulders. The black satin fabric fell to her waist, revealing her breasts.

Dominic's sharply indrawn breath broke the silence of the

room. He swiftly unbuttoned his shirt, fumbling with a few of the buttons as if his fingers refused to cooperate, and then ripped it off and flung it aside, leaving him naked. His thick arousal rose from a tangle of dark golden curls. A bead of moisture glistened on the tip.

She wet her lips, curled her fingers against the need to stroke him and turned her back. "Zip?"

She didn't hear him approach. Her first inkling that he had was the touch of his lips on her shoulder, and then his hands spanned her waist and slid up to cup her breasts. He rolled the tightened tips in his fingers. Desire coiled tightly between her legs. She leaned against him. His hard, hot erection pressed against her spine and his beard stubble erotically rasped her neck as he sipped a string of kisses on her skin. He murmured something in a language she couldn't understand.

She lifted a hand to cradle his face, stroke his bristly jaw and trace his soft, parted lips. She turned her head and whispered against his lips, "No fair. Speak English."

He ignored her request, lowered her zipper and pushed her dress from her hips. And then he pulled her flush against him and bound her close with his strong arms.

She'd miss this. His strength. His gentleness. His passion. The radiator-hot warmth of his hard body against her, surrounding her.

He stroked and caressed her, her breasts, her belly, her bottom and finally, the knot of need between her legs. Her muscles quivered with each deft stroke. She could barely stand. And then he scooped her into his arms and carried her to the bed. Madeline gasped. She'd never had a man literally sweep her off her feet. And she liked it.

She roped her arms around his neck and pulled him down with her. His thigh parted hers, but instead of taking her he lay beside her, burying his erection against her hip instead of inside her where she wanted it, needed it, craved it. She wanted him to hurry, but his hands mapped her body with slow precision, tracing each curve and indention, circling her aureole, her navel, her sex. She arched against him. He released her and twisted toward the nightstand.

Finally.

She expected to see a condom in his hand. Instead, the bracelet she'd admired at the market rested on his palm. Her heart clenched. "Dominic, you shouldn't have. But how did you…?"

"Ian purchased it for me. Accept this as a reminder of our time together."

How could she refuse? "Thank you."

She lifted her wrist. He slipped it on and then kissed each of her knuckles.

This feels like goodbye.

A knot formed in her throat and her pulse skipped with alarm. "Dominic, are you leaving tomorrow?"

"No departure date has been set." He sipped his way to her elbow, her shoulder, her neck. Madeline shoved aside her disquiet and lost herself in his passionate possession of her mouth. His hands seemed to be everywhere, arousing her, coaxing her, stroking her. She returned his embrace, sculpting the muscles of his shoulders, his back, his buttocks. His soft lips traveled over skin made more sensitive by the rasp of his evening beard.

Need spiraled inside her, coiling tighter and tighter until she squirmed beneath him. "Please."

He rose over her and eased inside her one tantalizing inch at a time. No condom, a corner of her mind insisted. But condoms didn't matter. She was protected. And she wanted to be as close to Dominic tonight as she possibly could be.

He withdrew and thrust deep. She countered his every move again and again until the tingles of orgasm, headier than that glass of expensive champagne, bubbled through her, racking her body with pleasure.

Dominic groaned her name against her neck and then crashed in her arms.

She held him tight.

And wasn't sure she ever wanted to let him go.

Madeline jolted upright in the bed.

Dominic's bed.

She shoved her tangled hair out of her face and blinked, trying to clear her groggy mind and her vision. What had woken her? She looked around. No clue.

Dominic's side. Empty. She smoothed a hand over the pillow. Cool. Checked the clock—11:00 a.m. She'd overslept. Oops.

A smile flitted across her lips. She'd had good reason for snoozing late. But now she'd have to hurry. Candace had a noon appointment with the bishop at St. Nicholas Cathedral and she wanted her wedding party to be there. That included Madeline.

Why hadn't Dominic woken her as he'd done every other morning? With kisses and caresses and slow and easy lovemaking? Because she'd forgotten to tell him about the church thing and it wasn't on the calendar she'd given him.

Unfamiliar masculine voices penetrated the closed bedroom door. She snatched the covers up to cover her nakedness.

Dominic had company. She had to get dressed.

Her dress lay draped across the back of the chair instead of puddled on the floor where he'd dropped it. Her panties, hair clip, purse and shoes sat in the chair. She tossed back the covers, raced toward her clothing, scooped up the bundle and ducked into the lavish bathroom only to skid to a halt.

Eeek. Her hair resembled a frizzy string mop and the remnants of her makeup looked hideous. She dumped her stuff on the counter, quickly braided her hair and then bent to wash her face. She brushed her teeth with her finger and a dab of Dominic's toothpaste. Better. Not great. Will have to do.

The bathroom light glinted on the bracelet. Her quick smile turned into a frown. Should she hide in here or leave?

Leave unless you want to arrive at the church looking like last night's leftovers.

She tugged on her clothing and stepped into her heels. The ensemble might have been fabulous last night, but at eleven in the morning it looked exactly like what it was—the outfit of a woman who'd spent the night.

"So," Madeline mumbled to herself, "how are you going to get out of the suite?"

The only entrance lay through the sitting room. Past Dominic and his visitors. In last night's wrinkled dress. Ugh.

She returned to the bedroom. She could still hear the voices, but it sounded as if the men had moved to the balcony—the balcony spanning the entire suite, including the bedroom. Her gaze darted to the window. Curtains closed. Whew.

The balcony. That could be good. She could slip out the front door while they were outside and maybe they wouldn't see her. Still, she listened at the bedroom door for a few seconds before daring to slowly twist the knob and ease the panel open a couple of cautious inches.

"Wedding preparations will begin at once," a male voice pronounced.

Wedding? Madeline peeked out the door. Dominic and two older men stood on the balcony. One, of perhaps sixty, had a thick head of silvered blond hair, Dominic's erect posture and bone structure. The other was older, more wizened looking. A little bent. Bald.

She scanned the rest of the room and slammed into Ian's dark stare. Her heart stuttered. He stood stiffly on the far side of the room. Uh-oh. Unless Dominic had told him, Ian hadn't known she was here. She put a finger to her lips in the universal "be quiet" symbol. He didn't respond with as much as a blink.

"And if I'm not ready to return?" Dominic asked. He wore last night's clothing, but his black shirt and pants didn't look as out of place as her cocktail dress. He hadn't shaved and his hair looked as if it had only been finger-combed.

"You knew that as soon as your bride was chosen you would have to return home," the thick-haired one replied.

Bride?

Madeline's world slowed to a standstill.

Bride? Her heart bolted into a racing rhythm. Dominic was getting married? To whom? Warmth—*hope*—filled her chest before she could stymie it.

Whoa. Where had that come from?

"I'm not ready. I need more time." Dominic again.

"Why? So you can play here with your paramour? I have seen the papers and heard the reports. Do you think I don't know where you were last night and with whom?" the regal guy asked.

Paramour. Madeline's brain snagged on the word and her stomach plunged.

Paramour. *Her.*

Not the bride in question. The strength seeped from her limbs. She leaned weakly against the doorjamb and closed her eyes. The tremor started deep inside and worked its way to her extremities.

What is your problem? You knew he wasn't going to marry you.

"I have promised to do as you wish, Father. I will take a bride. One of the council's choosing. But I need more time."

A bride of the council's choosing? Her confused brain couldn't make sense of that.

"Her family awaits your arrival," baldy said. "Promises have been made and agreements signed. The jet will fly you to Luxembourg this afternoon. Your father has brought your grandmother's engagement ring. You will propose tomorrow. A gala to announce and celebrate the engagement will take place next Saturday evening."

Nausea. Dizziness. Rapid heart rate. Cold, clammy hands. Shock, Madeline diagnosed. She struggled to inhale, but it hurt too much. Pain sliced through her like an explosion of surgical blades.

What had Dominic said that day in the café? He wasn't *committed to anyone at this time?* She remembered the exact words because she'd thought it an odd answer. As odd as him saying he wanted to share a bed for reasons other than duty, greed or fleeting attraction. She hadn't understood then. She did now.

He'd been planning to marry all along. A woman of some mysterious council's choosing.

She'd never been more to him than a way to pass the time while awaiting the name of his bride.

God, she hurt. Which made absolutely no sense.

Why? Why does it hurt so much?

Because, fool, you fell in love with him.

You knew this was temporary and that he was out of your reach. And you fell for him anyway.

She bit her lip to stop a whimper of pain. She loved him.

Did you expect him to marry a commoner like Prince Rainier did?

And what about virgins? Did you conveniently forget that Dominic, like Prince Charles, might have to marry a virgin?

Her hands fisted and her nails dug into her palms. At some point her subconscious must have started believing in fairy tales. Otherwise she wouldn't be feeling as if she'd been shoved off the deck of an ocean liner. Adrift. Drowning. Lost.

Ian. She suddenly remembered the unfriendly bodyguard. Her gaze found his. How often had he witnessed the crash of a woman's world? A woman who'd fallen in love with his unattainable boss.

Hurt and humiliated, she silently closed the door, staggered back into the bedroom and braced her arms on the desk. How could she sneak out when she could barely walk?

She couldn't face Dominic. Couldn't look into his eyes and know that the man she loved was destined to marry someone else.

One more pertinent fact he'd neglected to mention.

She'd been nothing more to him than a vacation fling. A no-strings-attached affair.

A half laugh, half sob burst from her lips. She shoved her fist against her mouth to stifle the pitiful sound. He'd given her *exactly* what she asked for. And it was breaking her heart.

He may have avoided full disclosure, but she was the one who'd set up the parameters and then screwed up and broken the rules by falling in love. Sucking in a fortifying breath, she squared her shoulders. She would never let him know how badly he'd hurt her.

She sank into the chair, yanked open the desk drawer and extracted a piece of hotel stationery and a pen. The pen slipped from her fingers. Twice. Her hands shook so badly she could barely put the tip to the page.

Pull it together before Dominic comes in here and finds you wrecked.

Gulping deep, painful breaths, she struggled for calm, the way she did when a heinous accident landed in her E.R.

She would not act like those shameless women who'd flung themselves at him at the ball. She wouldn't beg for crumbs of his attention. She had too much pride for that. And she would cling to what was left of her tattered pride until her last breath.

What she needed was a cool, emotionless, nonnegotiable goodbye. A final goodbye. Because she didn't want him to come looking for her. She couldn't bear a face-to-face encounter because she didn't think she could hide her feelings, and he would pity her if he figured out her secret. Or worse, he'd be patient and polite and detached—the way he'd been with the other women who'd made their availability so obvious.

Gritting her teeth, she formed each letter, each word, each painful phrase until she had nothing left to say. At least nothing she could or would print. And then she folded the stationery and rested her head on the desk.

Empty. She felt completely drained and empty inside.

As far as Dear Johns went, hers sucked. But she didn't have time for another draft. She straightened and shoved the note into an envelope. Her mouth was too dry to lick the seal, so she tucked in the flap and earned herself a paper cut for her trouble. She sucked the stinging wound.

How fitting that her goodbye left her cut and bleeding. Dominic had cut out her heart without even trying.

She stared at the bracelet. Should she leave it with the note? No. She wanted something to remind her not to put her trust in men. Each time she'd done so she'd been hurt.

The bedroom door opened. Startled, she sprang to her feet and spun around, clutching the letter to her chest.

Ian stepped inside and closed the door. His face showed no emotions. "I will show you out."

How many times had he said those words? "Do you always clean up his messes?"

"Dominic doesn't make messes."

She blinked in surprise. The man rarely spoke to her. She hadn't expected an answer. And Ian had used Dominic's name instead of his title. Progress. But too late.

He noted her cut, opened a dresser drawer, withdrew a white handkerchief and offered it to her.

Dominic's handkerchief. She carried it to her nose and inhaled a faint trace of his cologne and then wrapped it around her finger in a compression bandage. "How are you going to get me past Dominic's guests?"

"The Royal Suite has a hidden escape exit. Come with me." He stalked into the walk-in closet, bypassed Dominic's neatly hanging clothing and perfectly aligned shoes and twisted a fleur-de-lis at the base of the sconce light on the far wall. A panel slid sideways to reveal a dimly lit space beyond.

She edged forward, leaned in and looked at the shadowy area. "Where will this take me?"

"Follow the hall to the fire stairs."

So this was it. She was being shuffled out the back door like…a mistress. She gulped down tears of shame and loss and looked at the note in her hand. She should have left it on the desk.

"Would you give this to him?" She stabbed it toward Ian. After a moment's hesitation he accepted it. The guy didn't like her. Would he deliver her message?

Madeline cupped his hand with hers and looked into his dark eyes. "And, Ian, please, *please,* keep him safe."

Ten

"She's a child." Dominic stared at the photograph in dismay. "What will I have in common with such a baby?"

"She is nineteen. The same age as your first wife when you married," Ricardo, the Minister of State and senior council member said as he laid three more photographs of the pale blonde on the glass-topped balcony table. "Young enough to bear many heirs."

Disgust rolled through Dominic. It wasn't the girl's fault. She was attractive enough, but far too young for his tastes. He preferred mature women. Women who weren't too shy, insecure or inexperienced to speak their minds. Women like Madeline.

He looked over his shoulder at the closed bedroom door. Time had run out. He'd have to tell Madeline the truth and then say goodbye. He wouldn't get to show her Paris or Venice as planned. An odd sensation of panic bound his chest, making it difficult to breath.

His gaze returned to the picture in his hand. He'd always known his obligations to Montagnarde took precedence over his personal wishes. He led a privileged life, but those privileges came at a price. "Have I ever met her?"

"Twice, she says."

He had no recollection of either occasion. This young woman had made no impression on him whatsoever. That did not bode well for their future. And yet he was expected to marry her, bed her, impregnate her. The sooner the better.

His father placed a hand on his shoulder. "Love will come, Dominic. It did for your mother and I and for each of your sisters. It did with Giselle." His fingers tightened, released. "Ricardo and I are in need of sustenance. We will adjourn to the dining room downstairs. Clean up and join us."

The pair left, the suite door clicking shut behind them. Their bodyguards would be waiting outside. Only Dominic's insistence had kept Ian present for this confidential meeting. Matters such as this required the utmost discretion.

Dominic faced the bedroom door with a growing sense of dread. When Ian's knock had awoken him this morning, Dominic had not suspected the upheaval about to take place. And then Ian had informed him that his father was in the elevator and on the way upstairs. The weight of Dominic's responsibilities had crashed down on him. His father's arrival had been a surprise—an unpleasant one. For the king's arrival could only indicate two things. The end of Dominic's freedom. The end of his days with Madeline.

He glanced at his wrist and realized he'd failed to don his watch in his haste to dress and get out of his room before his father entered. Since Giselle's death his father had adopted the habit of sitting in Dominic's room at the palace and discussing the upcoming day's events while Dominic dressed.

Dominic hadn't wanted to expose Madeline to the embarrassment of his father barging into the room.

He shoved a hand through his hair. He wouldn't be able to wake Madeline with leisurely lovemaking this morning as he had each day for the past week. And once he told her the truth the best interlude of his life would be over.

Over.

His future committed to someone else.

The choking sensation intensified. He tugged at his already loose collar to no avail. Loss mired his steps as he approached the bedroom. He braced himself, turned the knob, pushed open the door.

The bed was empty, the bathroom dark. He entered, searching for her hiding place. "Madeline? You can come out. They're gone."

"She is not here, Dominic," Ian said behind him.

Dominic glanced at the digital clock on the nightstand and exhaled. She usually sneaked out at dawn, but not this morning. He smiled, but the smile vanished when he realized there would be no more sunrises with Madeline.

"She's gone."

The finality of Ian's words made the back of Dominic's neck prickle and his stomach tense. "How?"

"There is an emergency exit. I showed her the way."

"Why have I never been told of this exit?"

"I feared what you would do with the knowledge." Ian offered him an envelope bearing the Hôtel Reynard insignia in the upper left corner. "She overheard your conversation with your father and the Minister of State."

Dominic closed his eyes, clenched his teeth and let his head fall back. She should have heard the words from him. Exhaling a pent-up breath, he extracted the letter and read.

Dominic

Thank you for making my vacation memorable.

I'll be swamped with wedding duties over the next week. No time for fun and games or distractions.

You were great. Just what the doctor ordered. But like any prescription, this one has run its course.

I hate goodbyes, so this is the only one you'll get.

Goodbye.

I wish you the best.

Madeline

Pain swamped him like a tsunami. He called on numbness, his familiar companion in years past, but it refused to come. He swallowed once and then again. His hands fisted, the letter crumpling in his grip.

Madeline deserved the truth. The whole truth. She needed to know how important she was to him. How magnificent a lover. How good a friend. And he had to explain why he must say goodbye. She would understand. He would make her understand. "Where is she?"

"I don't know."

"What do you mean you don't know?"

"Fernand was excused from his duty while Mademoiselle Spencer *supposedly* spent the night on the yacht. In my urgency to remove her from the suite this morning I did not call him to track her when she left this room. I assumed she would return to her suite. She did not."

"She can't have gone far. I have her passport."

"It appears both of you went missing last night which proves my point about the secret exit. I am too old for shenanigans like this, Dominic."

Censure tainted Ian's voice. Censure Dominic deserved. "She treats me like a man, Ian. Not a future king."

Ian nodded sympathetically. "I know, but you have your destiny. And if you insist on putting yourself in danger I will not be able to do what Mademoiselle Spencer asked of me. Keep you safe."

Dominic's head jerked up. He searched Ian's eyes. "She didn't leave cursing me for my deception?"

"I cannot read the woman's mind. But she was not swearing or throwing things."

"Find her."

"Dominic, perhaps it is best to let things be."

"Find her." And when Ian didn't move, Dominic added, "That is a royal command."

Ian snapped to attention, pivoted sharply and headed toward the door. Dominic had never spoken to him as harshly.

"She ran," Dominic called after him. Ian stopped without turning. "Why did she run, Ian? Madeline Spencer is no coward. She is courageous and mouthy and she fights back. The Madeline I've come to love would have been in my face and reprimanding me for another lie of omission."

His heart slammed against his ribs like a ship against an iceberg, winding him, chilling him. *Love.*

He loved her.

He loved her sassy mouth. Her earthy sensuality. Her refusal to kowtow. He loved the way she listened to his plans for Montagnarde and added her own suggestions.

He loved her. And he couldn't have her. Agreements had been signed. Promises made. Breaking them could cause an international incident.

Ian slowly turned, looking as if he, too, were shocked by Dominic's discovery.

"Why would she run?" he repeated.

"Perhaps she does not wish to engage in a losing battle, Your Highness."

Dominic didn't believe that. There had to be more. But what? He straightened the crumpled page and studied it more closely. What wasn't she saying? Despite the bland note, he knew she had feelings for him. She'd shown it in countless ways in bed and out. She'd ended things far too easily.

Dominic rubbed a hand over his bristly jaw and tried to decipher the puzzle of Madeline Spencer. Too courageous to run, replayed in his head. And then the pieces of the puzzle slid into place.

She'd only had one other lover. A man she'd believed she loved. Could she possibly love him, Dominic wondered? He could not leave Monaco without finding out.

"She would only run if it hurt too much to say goodbye," he told Ian. He ripped off his shirt. "I must shower and join my father. I want Mademoiselle Spencer found and in my suite when I return. If she wants to say goodbye, then she'll have to say it to my face."

"I need you to hide me," Madeline said as soon as she, Candace and Vincent reached the shadowy alcove of the cathedral.

"What?" Candace asked.

"Just for the rest of the day." She fussed with the buttons on the dress she'd bought in a nearby boutique rather than risk returning to her suite.

"Come again?" Vincent stood to her right presenting her with his unscarred left side. Candace said the wounds he'd sustained in the pit fire still bothered him despite the numerous plastic surgeries which had reduced the severity of his scars.

"I need to hide from Prince Dominic of Montagnarde and his henchmen," she whispered.

Candace straightened to her full five feet three inches. "Did that jerk hurt you because if he did, I'll—"

"Have you done something illegal?" Vincent interrupted.

How like a man to cut to the chase, dealing with the facts rather than the emotions. "I haven't broken any laws, and Dominic didn't hurt me. He did exactly what I asked him to do. He gave me great sex and a memorable vacation."

"But?" Candace prompted.

Madeline scrunched her eyes. Candace possessed the stubbornness of a mule. If Madeline wanted her cooperation it would cost her. The truth.

"I fell in love with him."

Candace squealed and bounced in her sandals.

"Keep it down, for crying out loud. We're in a church," Madeline whispered. "And do not say 'I told you so.' I'm a little too raw for that right now."

"But this is great!"

Vincent shifted on his feet and looked back toward the others gathered in the cathedral as if he'd rather be anywhere except the middle of a girlie tête-à-tête.

"No, it's not great. He's flying off to meet his fiancée this afternoon."

Candace's smile morphed into a fierce scowl. "He's engaged? The lying two-timing royal rat."

"He wasn't committed to anyone else until today." Madeline honestly believed that. "From what I overheard I gather some committee or other has been searching for an acceptable princess-to-be. Now they've found her. And he's going to marry her." Just saying the words made her throat feel as raw as if she had a full-blown case of strep.

She grabbed Candace's and Vincent's hands. "I won't let you down with my wedding duties, but until Dominic is gone I need to stay out of sight. And I can't do that by myself. I don't know the language and I don't know the country."

"I'll handle it," Vincent said without hesitation.

"Thank you." Madeline's eyes burned, but she blinked back the tears. If one seeped through she feared a torrent would follow.

One day. She only had to get through one more day. And then Dominic would be gone and she could lose herself in Candace's wedding preparations until she returned home.

She would have laughed if she weren't afraid it would turn into hysteria. She'd come to Monaco wanting to avoid the wedding preparations. Now she wanted to bury herself in them and occupy her every thought with marriage minutiae so she wouldn't have time to think of what she'd never have with Dominic or anyone else. Because this time her heart had sustained too much damage to ever recover.

The dining room was crowded. Too crowded for what Dominic had to say.

He stopped beside his father's table, but waved away the waiter who rushed forward to pull back his chair. Instead he slipped him a large tip and asked him, "Would you please have our luncheon served in the suite?"

"Certainly, Your Highness." The man hustled toward the kitchen.

"Dominic, what is the meaning of this?" his father asked.

"I have something to say and you don't want me to say it here."

"Your Highness," Ricardo began, but Dominic silenced him with a frown. The councilman, who'd risen at Dominic's approach, shifted on his feet and looked to his king for guidance.

Dominic's father rose. "Very well, son. If we must."

The return to the suite passed in tense silence due to the presence of other hotel guests in the elevator. Dominic recognized Derek Reynard, the owner and CEO of the world-renowned Reynard Hotel chain, and his wife. It was the perfect opportunity for Dominic to introduce himself and ask for a meeting to discuss the construction of a Hôtel Reynard in Montagnarde, but he had more important matters to deal with at the moment. The couple turned toward Madeline's suite. He wanted to follow, but first he had to deal with more critical issues.

The moment Ian closed the suite door behind them, Dominic faced his father. "I cannot marry the girl the council has chosen."

The minister sputtered. Dominic feared the septuagenarian might have a heart attack.

Dominic's father tensed, but otherwise showed no reaction. "Why not?"

"Because the woman I love is here in Monaco."

"And what of your duty to the crown?"

"I willingly serve my country, but I should not be cursed with an indifferent marriage due to a three-hundred-year-old custom. That custom, like our economy, needs modernizing."

"What of the agreements, Your Highness?" Ricardo asked. "The negotiations?"

"I'll renounce my title, if my decision causes difficulties for Montagnarde, but I will not marry that child or any other the council selects. I would rather live in exile than spend my life with a woman I care nothing about. I'm not a stud whose sole purpose is to service a mare."

"You would leave your family and your country for this woman you've been consorting with during your stay in Monaco?" his father asked.

"Yes, sir. I prefer to live happily elsewhere with Madeline than miserably at home without her."

"Doing what, Dominic? How will you support yourself and your wife if you leave your title and fortune behind?"

"I have the qualifications and connections to find work in the hotel industry."

His father's eyebrows rose. "You would work as a commoner? Draw a salary. Pay a mortgage?"

"Yes."

"What of your plans to develop Montagnarde's tourist potential?"

"I would mourn the loss of my dream, but not as much I would regret losing Madeline. I have dedicated the past fifteen years of my life to the betterment of Montagnarde. My plan is a sound one, and with or without me you should pursue it. But I would walk away from it all in an instant for her."

"What makes you think she's worthy of becoming a queen?"

"She's intelligent and courageous and doesn't have an obsequious bone in her body. She doesn't care about my title or wealth, and she fights me for the check after dinner. She calls me the most hideous names." Your Royal Beefcake, His Serene Sexiness and Sir Lickalot were but a few. The memories brought a smile to his lips.

His father's eyes narrowed speculatively. "She's never married?"

Dominic sucked a surprised breath at the question which cracked open the door to possibility.

Ian cleared his throat, drawing the king's attention. "Your Majesty, if I may speak?" He waited for acknowledgment. "I have the full report on Mademoiselle Spencer if you wish to peruse it."

The king made a go-ahead motion with his hand and Ian

left the room and returned with a folder. He opened it and read, "Madeline Marie Spencer, thirty-two, has never married although she has had one long engagement. She has no children, graduated near the top of her university class and is currently employed as a physician's assistant in a trauma center in Charlotte, North Carolina, U.S.A., where she is well-respected by her peers. Her credit rating is excellent, her personal debt minimal, and she has no criminal record. Not even a parking ticket. Her father, a policeman, is deceased and her mother is a retired schoolteacher."

"Where is she, this paragon?" Dominic's father asked.

"She has not been located, Your Majesty, since she left the hotel this morning. At Prince Dominic's request, we are searching."

Dominic's frustration level rose. He had to find her.

"I would like to meet this woman who has mesmerized my son in such a short time. When she's found bring her here." His attention returned to Dominic. "This will not be without complications, you understand?"

Adrenaline pulsed through Dominic's system at his father's acceptance. "I do."

"She has accepted your suit?"

"I have not been free to state my intentions."

"But, Your Majesty, the agreements… This could cause a diplomatic scandal," Ricardo protested.

Dominic's father held up a hand to silence him. "My son has had enough unhappiness in his life, Ricardo. Dominic and I will deal with the agreements. We will fly to Luxembourg this afternoon to personally make our apologies and any reparations required." He turned back to Dominic. "You're sure she's the one?"

"I've never been more certain of anything in my life."

"And do you believe she will accept your proposal?"

Tension invaded his limbs. "I don't know, Papa. But if I can't have Madeline I don't want anyone else."

"I don't know why you couldn't just use your passkey and take Madeline's passport from Dominic's room safe," Candace whispered to Vincent in the hallway of the American Consulate on Tuesday afternoon.

"Because it's stealing," Vincent replied patiently for the third time. "The hotel cannot afford the reputation of violating its guests."

"But it's *hers*."

"Stop," Madeline interjected. "As much as I love you, Candace, Vincent's right. We can't go digging around the safe just because we *think* my passport might be there. I've reported it lost and the consulate guys have promised to put a rush on it. I should have a replacement before I fly home on Sunday."

Madeline leaned against the wall beside the exit while Vincent stepped outside and signaled the waiting car. She slid on her new oversize Jackie-O sunglasses and covered her hair with a silk scarf. Disguised like a fugitive and her only crime was falling for the wrong guy.

She grimaced. "I can't believe Dominic didn't check out of the hotel. Why is he keeping the suite? Is he coming back? I can't go on riding in the floorboard of Vincent's car and hiding at his apartment."

Candace squeezed her hand. "You have no choice. Dominic had that Fernand guy following you. You had to disappear. You'll only be riding in floorboards and sneaking up service elevators for a few more days."

"But you had to reschedule everything except the wedding and rehearsal party because Dominic had my schedule."

"Like that's the worst catastrophe to ever befall a bride. Jeez, get over it, Madeline. I've said it's not a big deal."

But it was a big deal. Candace had enough stress dealing with planning a wedding in a foreign country. She didn't need the additional pressure of shuffling times and meeting places at the last minute because of Madeline's mistake.

"Maybe I should just see him and get it over with when he returns. *If* he returns."

She hoped it wouldn't kill her. God knows, losing Mike had never hurt like this. But then she'd realized in the three days since her affair with Dominic had ended that Mike's defection had hurt her pride not her heart. She'd been more concerned with what her coworkers thought of her for being so easily duped than with Mike's leaving.

She hadn't loved Mike. Not the way she loved Dominic.

Not once had she pictured herself growing old with Mike. She'd focused more on the house and children they'd have and thought more about being a mother than a wife. Not so with Dominic. She'd miss waking up beside him, making love with him and listening to his aspirations in the darkness. She'd miss his stupid little bows, the way he could melt her with his smile and his loyalty to the hulking Ian. Children? Oh yeah, a few little princes and princesses would have been nice, too, but Dominic was the main attraction.

"No, you won't confront him," Candace interrupted her pity party. "There's no reason to put yourself through that. And he might have *her* with him."

Madeline flinched. Good point. She didn't really want to come face-to-face with the woman who would be living *her* dream.

"Your Dear John generously gave him an easy out—which is more than he deserved, if you ask me. I think you should have skewered his nuts and roasted them over the barbecue." Candace held up her hands. "I know. I know. He made no promises. I got the stringless affair part the first time you explained it. And even though I thought it was a dumb idea, I really thought he was the right guy for you, Madeline. I've never seen you as happy. And I'm seriously peeved over being wrong."

At Vincent's signal Madeline and Candace raced to the car stopped by the curb and scooted in, and then Vincent turned around and looked at Madeline over the back of the seat. Her stomach sank at his serious expression.

"The hotel called. Rossi's back."

Eleven

Twenty-four more hours and she'd be gone.

Madeline kept to the outer fringes of the large private garden housing the wedding reception. An hour ago she'd completed her bridesmaid duties. The happy couple had danced their first dance and cut the cake. By this time tomorrow Madeline would be winging her way back to the States.

She didn't understand why Dominic was still looking for her unless it was to return her passport—an item he could easily leave at the hotel's front desk. Last night he'd shown up uninvited at the posh Italian Restaurant where the dinner following Candace and Vincent's civil service had been held and demanded to speak to her. Luckily, Madeline had spotted him before he'd seen her, and she'd been able to make a hasty exit out a side door through the kitchens and into the back alley.

Today she'd been so tense during the religious ceremony

at the cathedral that she'd barely heard the service. She'd kept expecting Dominic to burst through the doors, and she'd startled at every sound. She felt guilty as hell for tainting her friend's special event with unpleasant thoughts, but Candace, bless her, was taking Madeline's distraction in stride.

During the past week Madeline had adopted Amelia's habit of watching entertainment TV and reading the English tabloid papers. She kept waiting for news of Dominic's engagement to break.

Wait a minute.

Madeline dropped the leaf she'd been folding like sloppy origami. According to what she'd overheard in Dominic's suite last Saturday, the official announcement of his engagement would be made tonight at a gala in Luxembourg. Loss weighted her stomach and goose bumps crept over her skin despite the sunny day and comfortable temperatures. She hugged her silk stole around her bare shoulders.

If Dominic was there, he couldn't be here. Right?

Right.

So she didn't need to hide out here in the dappled shade of the lemon trees. She could rejoin the party and celebrate her friend's happiness.

She could even find it in her battered heart to be happy for Mike because he'd deserved more than the indifferent emotion—Dominic had diagnosed her failed engagement well—Madeline had offered. And her feelings for Mike had been indifferent, she admitted, because she'd held back and never fully committed her heart. He was still a jerk for cheating, but part of the failure of their relationship rested squarely on her shoulders.

Picking up her discarded bouquet from the stone bench, she made her way back across the flagstones to the center of the patio and stopped by Candace's side. Her friend's radiant smile faded and a worried look took its place.

Madeline hugged her. "Don't look like that. I am happy for you. Both of you."

And she meant it. Just because her dreams hadn't come true didn't mean she couldn't be thrilled her friends' had.

Candace took her hand. "You know I love you, right?"

Madeline stiffened. The back of her neck prickled. Why did that sound ominous? "Candace...?"

Madeline shot an anxious glance toward the château and spotted Makos. Her breath left in a whoosh. She turned toward the back corner of the garden where she'd been hiding, and saw Fernand yards away from her hiding spot. She then saw Ian in the opposite corner. Panic fluttered in her belly and squeezed her lungs. She spun left, right, searching for an exit, but every escape route had been blocked by a bodyguard. Members of the royal security team wore blank faces and had stiff bearings. Her years of exposure to law enforcement officers made them easy for her to pick out of the crowd.

Gulp.

"Dominic's here," she croaked.

Candace's fingers tightened. "Yes."

Bewildered, Madeline stared at her friend and tried to comprehend the betrayal.

She had to get out of here.

Toby blocked her path, parked a big paw on her shoulder. "Hear him out, Madeline. And then if you still want me to, I'll beat the crap out of him."

Madeline scanned the faces around her. Amelia and Toby, Candace and Vincent, Stacy and Franco. Were they all in on this? She clenched her teeth on a panicked, furious cry.

The bodyguards closed in until she was surrounded by a circle of dark-suited men. Three she could handle. A dozen? Probably not. Her heart raced, her mouth dried and adrenaline flooded her bloodstream.

Run, her conscience screamed.

No, dammit, I am no coward. I am through running.

But I can't let him know how much he's hurt me.

Madeline closed her eyes, inhaled deeply and exhaled slowly, fighting to still the tremors racking her. When she lifted her lids Dominic stood inside the circle and only two yards away. He wore a black suit with what she now recognized as Montagnarde's gold crest on the breast and a white open-collared shirt. His brushed-back hair accentuated his smooth-shaven jaw, but beneath his tan his face looked pale. A thin, white line rimmed his mouth and his blue eyes stared somberly into hers.

The silver-haired man, Dominic's father, stood to Dominic's right, the bald guy to his left.

"Why aren't you in Luxembourg?" she choked out.

"Father, this is the woman who held a knife to my throat and threatened my life," Dominic announced clearly, distinctly and loud enough for the crowd surrounding them to hear.

The guests' gasps barely registered. Why would he cause a scene? He knew how much she hated publicity. Madeline lifted her chin. "Tattletale. You asked for it."

Dominic's father stepped forward. "Mademoiselle, in Montagnarde threatening the life of a monarch is a serious offense."

That wasn't news. She narrowed her eyes. She looked from one man to the other. Why were they replaying this?

"There is only one way to commute the sentence," the bald guy said. "The accused must look the victim in the eye and swear she doesn't love him."

Her heart stopped. In a second someone was going to have to start CPR. But then her heart spontaneously jolted back into rhythm which meant she had to live through this instead of conveniently dying of mortification.

She sought Dominic's gaze. How could he ask that of her? How could he publicly humiliate her this way? "And if I refuse to participate in this ridiculous charade?"

Posture erect and looking totally regal, he closed the gap between them, stopping a foot away. "You stole from me, Madeline Spencer."

Confused, she blinked and shook her head. "Ian gave me that handkerchief and you bought me this bracelet. I never took anything else."

"You took the most important thing." His eyes and mouth softened. "You took my heart."

She gasped and struggled to make sense of his words. Was this a cruel joke? Was he going to marry his princess and ask Madeline to be his mistress or something? She glanced at Candace and saw tears streaming down her friend's smiling face.

She turned back to Dominic. "What about your bride-to-be? The one the council chose? The one who's supposed to wear your grandmother's ring? The one you're supposed to get engaged to tonight, for Pete's sake?"

Dominic's gaze didn't waver. "I agreed to marry without love because I never believed I would find it again."

A smile lifted one corner of his mouth. He lifted a hand and cradled her face. She wanted so badly to lean into his touch that it took all her strength to jerk away.

"When you held that knife to my throat you changed my life, Madeline. I have never known a woman with your courage. No other woman treats me like a man instead of a monarch. And no other woman loves me as completely and unselfishly as you do."

She flinched. *He knew.* A lie of denial sprang to her lips, but the intense emotion in his eyes made her forget the words.

"Tell me I'm wrong, Madeline. Tell me you don't love me, and I'll walk away."

She wanted to believe. God, she wanted to believe what she thought he was saying. Her breath shuddered in and then out.

"I'm not a virgin. And you know it," she whispered.

His eyes twinkled with laughter. "Good thing that's not a requirement."

Her eyes and chest burned. She blinked rapidly to keep the tears—happy, hopeful tears—at bay and extended her arms, wrists together. "I guess you're going to have to cuff me and take me into custody. Because I can't lie."

Dominic's eyes widened. Surprise and happiness filled their depths and a brief smile flashed across his lips before he once more donned the serious mask. "Then I hereby sentence you to life, Madeline Spencer. Life with me."

He dropped to his knee and bowed his head. For a moment it looked as if he said a silent prayer. Then Dominic's gold-tipped lashes lifted and his bedroom blue eyes found hers. "Marry me, Madeline. Be my friend. My lover. My wife. And one day, my queen."

He reached into his pocket and withdrew an exquisite emerald ring in an antique-looking gold setting.

She pressed her trembling fingers to her lips. A warm tear slid over her fingertip. "You forgot your handcuffs?"

He grinned. "I promise I'll find them later if you say yes."

She looked at Dominic's father and found acceptance and even approval in his face. "You're okay with this? Clearly, I'm not princess material."

"I beg to differ, mademoiselle. Now give my son the answer he desires."

She stared into the face of the man she loved, the man who'd stolen her heart in a matter of moments. "I always thought I wanted an on-your-knees proposal. But I was wrong."

Uncertainty flickered in Dominic's eyes.

"It's not how the proposal is delivered that matters. It's who's asking the question." She caressed his cheek, cupped his smooth jaw and stroked a finger over his lips. "Get up, Dominic. I refuse to have this discussion unless we're eye-to-eye, face-to-face and heart-to-heart."

He slowly rose.

"You are such a romantic. I love it. And I love you." She rose on her tiptoes and brushed her lips to his. She tasted tears. "Yes, Dominic, I'll marry you."

His arms banded around her with crushing force and he lifted her off the ground. The crowd surrounding them let out a deafening cheer.

Dominic set her down and kissed her so gently her heart swelled to squeeze the air from her lungs. He pulled back a fraction and braced his forehead against hers. "I love you, Madeline."

He cradled her face, brushing her tears away with his thumbs. "I hope you know what you're getting into. Royal weddings are extravagant affairs."

Madeline laughed. She never thought she'd be grateful for those six wasted years. "I have a little wedding planning experience. As long as I have you, I can handle it."

* * * * *

Don't miss the conclusion of
MONTE CARLO AFFAIRS
Look for
THE PLAYBOY'S PASSIONATE PURSUIT
by Emilie Rose
Coming in August 2007
from Silhouette Desire

Every Life Has More
Than One Chapter™

Award-winning author Stevi Mittman delivers another
hysterical mystery, featuring Teddi Bayer, an irrepressible
heroine, and her to-die-for hero, Detective Drew Scoones.
After all, life on Long Island can be murder!

*Turn the page for a sneak peek
at the warm and funny fourth book,
WHOSE NUMBER IS UP, ANYWAY?
in the Teddi Bayer series,
by STEVI MITTMAN.
On sale August 7*

CHAPTER 1

"Before redecorating a room, I always advise my clients to empty it of everything but one chair. Then I suggest they move that chair from place to place, sitting in it, until the placement feels right. Trust your instincts when deciding on furniture placement. Your room should feel right."

—TipsFromTeddi.com

Gut feelings. You know, that gnawing in the pit of your stomach that warns you that you are about to do the absolute stupidest thing you could do? Something that will ruin life as you know it?

I've got one now, standing at the butcher counter in King Kullen, the grocery store in the same strip mall as L.I. Lanes, the bowling alley cum billiard parlor I'm in the process of redecorating for its "Grand Opening."

I realize being in the wrong supermarket probably doesn't sound exactly dire to you, but you aren't the one buying your father a brisket at a store your mother will somehow know isn't Waldbaum's.

And then, June Bayer isn't your mother.

The woman behind the counter has agreed to go into the freezer to find a brisket for me, since there aren't any in the case. There are packages of pork tenderloin, piles of spare ribs and rolls of sausage, but no briskets.

Warning Number Two, right? I should be so out of here.

But, no, I'm still in the same spot when she comes back out, brisketless, her face ashen. She opens her mouth as if she is going to scream, but only a gurgle comes out.

And then she pinballs out from behind the counter, knocking bottles of Peter Luger Steak Sauce to the floor on her way, now hitting the tower of cans at the end of the prepared foods aisle and sending them sprawling, now making her way down the aisle, careening from side to side as she goes.

Finally, from a distance, I hear her shout, "He's deeeeeeaaaad! Joey's deeeeeaaaad."

My first thought is *You should always trust your gut.*

My second thought is that now, somehow, my mother will know I was in King Kullen. For weeks I will have to hear "What did you expect?" as though whenever you go to King Kullen someone turns up dead. And if the detective investigating the case turns out to be Detective Drew Scoones...well, I'll never hear the end of that from her, either.

She still suspects I murdered the guy who was found dead on my doorstep last Halloween just to get Drew back into my life.

Several people head for the butcher's freezer and I position myself to block them. If there's one thing I've learned from finding people dead—and the guy on my doorstep wasn't the first one—it's that the police get very testy when you mess with their murder scenes.

"You can't go in there until the police get here," I say, stationing myself at the end of the butcher's counter and in front of the Employees Only door, acting as if I'm some sort of authority. "You'll contaminate the evidence if it turns out to be murder."

Shouts and chaos. You'd think I'd know better than to throw the word *murder* around. Cell phones are flipping open and tongues are wagging.

I amend my statement quickly. "Which, of course, it probably isn't. Murder, I mean. People die all the time, and it's not always in hospitals or their own beds, or…" I babble when I'm nervous, and the idea of someone dead on the other side of the freezer door makes me very nervous.

So does the idea of seeing Drew Scoones again. Drew and I have this on-again, off-again sort of thing…that I kind of turned off.

Who knew he'd take it so personally when he tried to get serious and I responded by saying we could talk about *us* tomorrow—and then caught a plane to my parents' condo in Boca the next day? In July. In the middle of a job.

For some crazy reason, he took that to mean that I was avoiding him and the subject of *us*.

That was three months ago. I haven't seen him since.

The manager, who identifies himself and points to his nameplate in case I don't believe him, says he has to go into *his cooler*. "Maybe Joey's not dead," he says. "Maybe he can be saved, and you're letting him die in there. Did you ever think of that?"

In fact, I hadn't. But I had thought that the murderer might try to go back in to make sure his tracks were covered, so I say that I will go in and check.

Which means that the manager and I couple up and go in together while everyone pushes against the doorway to peer in, erasing any chance of finding clean prints on that Employee Only door.

I expect to find carcasses of dead animals hanging from hooks, and maybe Joey hanging from one, too. I think it's going to be very creepy and I steel myself, only to find a rather benign series of shelves with large slabs of meat laid out carefully on them, along with boxes and boxes marked simply Chicken.

Nothing scary here, unless you count the body of a middle-aged man with graying hair sprawled faceup on the floor. His eyes are wide open and unblinking. His shirt is stiff. His pants are stiff. His body is stiff. And his expression, you should forgive the pun—is frozen. Bill-the-manager crosses himself and stands mute while I pronounce the guy dead in a sort of *happy now?* tone.

"We should not be in here," I say, and he nods his head emphatically and helps me push people out of the doorway just in time to hear the police sirens and see the cop cars pull up outside the big store windows.

Bobbie Lyons, my partner in Teddi Bayer Interior Designs (and also my neighbor, my best friend and my private fashion police), and Mark, our carpenter (and my dogsitter, confidant, and ego booster), rush in from next door. They beat the cops by a half step and shout out my name. People point in my direction.

After all the publicity that followed the unfortunate incident during which I shot my ex-husband, Rio Gallo, and then the subsequent murder of my first client—which I solved, I might add—it seems like the whole world, or at least all of Long Island, knows who I am.

Mark asks if I'm all right. (Did I remember to mention that the man is drop-dead-gorgeous-but-a-decade-too-young-for-me-yet-too-old-for-my-daughter-thank-god?) I don't get a chance to answer him because the police are quickly closing in on the store manager and me.

"The woman—" I begin telling the police. Then I have to pause for the manager to fill in her name, which he does: *Fran.*

I continue. "Right. Fran. Fran went into the freezer to get a brisket. A moment later she came out and screamed that Joey was dead. So I'd say she was the one who discovered the body."

"And you are…?" the cop asks me. It comes out a bit like who do I *think* I am, rather than who am I really?

"An innocent bystander," Bobbie, hair perfect, makeup just right, says, carefully placing her body between the cop and me.

"And she was just leaving," Mark adds. They each take one of my arms.

Fran comes into the inner circle surrounding the cops. In case it isn't obvious from the hairnet and bloodstained white apron with Fran embroidered on it, I explain that she was the butcher who was going for the brisket. Mark and Bobbie take that as a signal that I've done my job and they can now get me out of there. They twist around, with me in the middle, as if we're a Rockettes line, until we are facing away from the butcher counter. They've managed to propel me a few steps toward the exit when disaster—in the form of a Mazda RX7 pulling up at the loading curb—strikes.

Mark's grip on my arm tightens like a vise. "Too late," he says.

Bobbie's expletive is unprintable. "Maybe there's a back door," she suggests, but Mark is right. It's too late.

I've laid my eyes on Detective Scoones. And while my gut is trying to warn me that my heart shouldn't go there, regions farther south are melting at just the sight of him.

"Walk," Bobbie orders me.

And I try to. Really.

Walk, I tell my feet. *Just put one foot in front of the other.*

I can do this because I know, in my heart of hearts, that if Drew Scoones was still interested in me, he'd have gotten in touch with me after I returned from Boca. And he didn't.

Since he's a detective, Drew doesn't have to wear one of

those dark blue Nassau County Police uniforms. Instead, he's got on jeans, a tight-fitting T-shirt and a tweedy sports jacket. If you think that sounds good, you should see him. Chiseled features, cleft chin, brown hair that's naturally a little sandy in the front, a smile that…well, that doesn't matter. He isn't smiling now.

He walks up to me, tucks his sunglasses into his breast pocket and looks me over from head to toe.

"Well, if it isn't Miss Cut and Run," he says. "Aren't you supposed to be somewhere in Florida or something?" He looks at Mark accusingly, as if he was covering for me when he told Drew I was gone.

"Detective Scoones?" one of the uniforms says. "The stiff's in the cooler and the woman who found him is over there." He jerks his head in Fran's direction.

Drew continues to stare at me.

You know how when you were young, your mother always told you to wear clean underwear in case you were in an accident? And how, a little farther on, she told you not to go out in hair rollers because you never knew who you might see—or who might see you? And how now your best friend says she wouldn't be caught dead without makeup and suggests you shouldn't either?

Okay, today, *finally,* in my overalls and Converse sneakers, I get it.

I brush my hair out of my eyes. "Well, I'm back," I say. As if he hasn't known my exact whereabouts. The man is a detective, for heaven's sake. "Been back awhile."

Bobbie has watched the exchange and apparently decided she's given Drew all the time he deserves. "And we've got work to do, so…" she says, grabbing my arm and giving Drew a little two-fingered wave goodbye.

As I back up a foot or two, the store manager sees his chance and places himself in front of Drew, trying to get his attention. Maybe what makes Drew such a good detective is his ability to focus.

Only what he's focusing on is me.

"Phone broken? Carrier pigeon died?" he asks me, taking in Fran, the manager, the meat counter and that Employees Only door, all without taking his eyes off me.

Mark tries to break the spell. "We've got work to do there, you've got work to do here, Scoones," Mark says to him, gesturing toward next door. "So it's back to the alley for us."

Drew's lip twitches. "You working the alley now?" he says.

"If you'd like to follow me," Bill-the-manager, clearly exasperated, says to Drew—who doesn't respond. It's as if waiting for my answer is all he has to do.

So, fine. "You knew I was back," I say.

The man has known my whereabouts every hour of the day for as long as I've known him. And my mother's not the only one who won't buy that he "just happened" to answer this particular call. In fact, I'm willing to bet my children's lunch money that he's taken every call within ten miles of my home since the day I got back.

And now he's gotten lucky.

"*You* could have called *me,*" I say.

"You're the one who said *tomorrow* for our talk and then flew the coop, chickie," he says. "I figured the ball was in your court."

"Detective?" the uniform says. "There's something you ought to see in here."

Drew gives me a look that amounts to *in or out?*

He could be talking about the investigation, or about our relationship.

Bobbie tries to steer me away. Mark's fists are balled.

Drew waits me out, knowing I won't be able to resist what might be a murder investigation.

Finally he turns and heads for the cooler.

And, like a puppy dog, I follow.

Bobbie grabs the back of my shirt and pulls me to a halt.

"I'm just going to show him something," I say, yanking away.

"Yeah," Bobbie says, pointedly looking at the buttons on my blouse. The two at breast level have popped. "That's what I'm afraid of."

HARLEQUIN®

Mediterranean
NIGHTS™

*Glamour, elegance, mystery and revenge
aboard the high seas...*

Coming in August 2007...

THE TYCOON'S SON

by
award-winning author
Cindy Kirk

Businessman Theo Catomeris's long-estranged
father is determined to reconnect with his son, so
he hires Trish Melrose to persuade Theo to renew
his contract with Liberty Line. Sailing aboard the
luxurious *Alexandra's Dream* is a rare opportunity for
the single mom to mix business and pleasure. But
an undeniable attraction between Trish and Theo is
distracting her from the task at hand....

HM38962

HARLEQUIN®
Super Romance®

*Looking for a romantic, emotional
and unforgettable escape?*

*You'll find it this month and every month
with a Harlequin Superromance!*

Rory Gorenzi has a sense of humor and a sense of
honor. She also happens to be good with children.

Seamus Lee, widower and father of four, needs
someone with exactly those traits.

They meet at the Colorado mountain school owned
by Rory's father, where she teaches skiing and
avalanche safety. But Seamus—and his children—
learn more from her than that....

Look for

GOOD WITH CHILDREN

by Margot Early,

*available August 2007, and these other
fantastic titles from Harlequin Superromance.*

REQUEST YOUR FREE BOOKS!

2 FREE NOVELS PLUS 2 FREE GIFTS!

Passionate, Powerful, Provocative!

SDES07

REASONS FOR REVENGE

A brand-new provocative miniseries by *USA TODAY*
bestselling author **Maureen Child** begins with

SCORNED
BY THE BOSS

Jefferson Lyon is a man used to having his own way.
He runs his shipping empire from California, and
his admin Caitlyn Monroe runs the rest of his world.
When Caitlin decides she's had enough and needs
new scenery, Jefferson devises a plan to get her back.
Jefferson *never* loses, but little does he know that
he's in a competition....

Don't miss any of the other titles from the
REASONS FOR REVENGE trilogy by
USA TODAY bestselling author **Maureen Child.**

SCORNED BY THE BOSS #1816
Available August 2007

SEDUCED BY THE RICH MAN #1820
Available September 2007

CAPTURED BY THE BILLIONAIRE #1826
Available October 2007

Only from Silhouette Desire!

COMING NEXT MONTH

SDCNM0707